ECHOES OF DEATH

JANET HARWARD

Janet Harward lives in the West Midlands with her husband and two daughters. Her first novel, *Murder on The English Riviera,* was published in 1995, and was followed in 1996 by *The Teddy Bear Murders*, the first Josephine Blake mystery, and *In Memory of Murder,* the second Josephine Blake mystery. *Echoes of Death* is the latest in the Josephine Blake series.

Also by Janet Harward

Murder on the English Riviera
The Teddy Bear Murders
In Memory of Murder

JANET HARWARD

ECHOES OF DEATH

O'Neill Publishing

First published in Great Britain by O'Neill Publishing, 1998.
This edition 1998 O'Neill Publishing.

A CIP catalogue record for this book is available from the British Library.

ISBN 0-9525161-3-6

9 8 7 6 5 4 3 2 1

Book design and Typography by Crow Media Design.
Printed and bound in Great Britain by Caledonian International Book Manufacturing Ltd, Glasgow.

This book is set in Torbay in Devon. Most district names are genuine. Some places are fictional. The characters and situations are entirely imaginary and bear no relation to any real person or happening.

Dedication

For Sarah and Christina, of whom I am so proud.

Acknowledgements

The author wishes to thank Chief Superintendent Malcolm Ross (West Midlands Police) for his help in writing this book.

In writing this book I used many books as research, but especially *Jack the Ripper, 100 Years Investigation* by Terence Sharkey, Ward Lock Ltd., London.

For people seriously interested in 'Saucy Jack' and his crimes, *The Whitechapel Review* is available from Stephen Wright, PO Box 1341, FDR Station, New York, NY10150-1341, USA

ECHOES OF DEATH

Chapter 1

JANE FIELDING FELT OLDER than her thirty-two years, as she stood in front of the brightly-lit mirror in the ladies powder room. The harshness of the fluorescent tube showed every line and wrinkle of her face giving it a sallow glow. She brushed her short brown hair and dabbed make-up beneath her eyes in an attempt to conceal the dark shadows. Finally, after applying a fresh coat of lipstick, she stood back from the full length mirror as she straightened her short black skirt and inspected herself. Her face might need some work these days, but she had the firm and trim body of a woman ten years younger.

'Mmm... not a bad figure for your age, old gal,' she thought. *'Still, I think I'd better invest in some anti-wrinkle cream.'*

As she opened the door to leave, a group of young women in their twenties pushed past her, nearly knocking her over. They were giggling and shouting, obviously the worse for drink.

Jane walked across the dance floor of the Black Cat nightclub, searching for the man she'd met some thirty minutes earlier, who'd said he'd get her a drink. Suddenly she caught sight of him at the crowded bar, holding a glass in each hand.

Little did she know as she approached him, her looks were the least of her troubles.

* * *

The sex was unbelievably good. Whether this was because she hadn't slept with anyone for over two years, or whether his technique in love making was as good as he thought it was, Jane wasn't sure. All she knew was she hadn't had so much fun in a long time. This may have been the reason she didn't object when he produced a pair of handcuffs, and suggested they use them. She was a little apprehensive, but thought *'What the heck! It's a bit of excitement.'*

After they'd had sex for the second time, he sat on the edge of the bed and lit a cigarette.

"I need the loo," she said. "Can you get these things off me?"

He started to laugh.

"Oh come on, I'm desperate – I'll wet the bed otherwise."

He came towards the top of the bed as if to undo them, but to her horror put his hands around her neck, and started to press her throat gently.

Then he stopped and smiled.

Jane started to laugh, she'd had quite a lot to drink, and in her pleasantly muzzy state she thought it was all part of the sexual game. She had read somewhere that slight strangulation increased the pleasure of orgasm.

As he put his hands around her neck for the second time, he applied more pressure.

She found it difficult to breathe, and started to choke. She was waiting for him to stop, as her face was turning blue, but he didn't.

Terrified, her heart pounded in her ears. Her slight sheen of sweat from the earlier sex now felt cold and clammy. She was completely helpless, and the only way she could defend herself was to kick out, as she writhed frantically from side to side, the handcuffs clanging against the brass head bed. Finally a stray, sharp kick caught him in the genitals, and he fell back in pain, cupping his hands between his legs.

He was stunned for a moment or so, but she knew it was hopeless.

When he'd recovered and the pain had subsided, he sat up and smiled at her. His eyes shone with an evil malevolence.

"I like a woman with spirit. It's more fun when they put up a fight."

Jane relaxed a little. *'Perhaps it's just a game to him, a bit of sick perverted fun, and he'll unshackle me,'* she thought.

She was wrong. He tormented her for a further hour, before he finally squeezed the last breath of life from her body.

Before mutilating her with a knife.

Chapter 2

AS JOSEPHINE WALKED from the darkness of the courtroom and down the steps of the court buildings, she held her hand up to shield her eyes from the strong sunlight. After fumbling in her handbag for a moment or so, she managed to find her sunglasses. They would have a dual purpose – not just shading her eyes from the sun, but also hiding the tears that were welling up inside them.

Her emotions were confused; part of her felt relieved that the weeks of wrangling with lawyers on how the house and possessions should be divided was finally settled. The animosity and bitterness between Tom and herself had subsided to some degree, leaving them at least on speaking terms, though not exactly friends. Simultaneously she felt desperately sad. She had known for some years that divorce was inevitable, but had hoped she could remain friends with the man she had spent the last twenty years with, and be able to call on him if she ever felt the need. Despite her independent front, Josephine wasn't as self reliant a woman as she portrayed herself.

Making her way towards the car park, she felt alone, and wished she hadn't rejected offers from her daughter Jessica, and her friends to come to court with her for support. All she wanted to do was get home as quickly as possible. Her body trembled and she felt emotionally exhausted. Over the years, due to her profession in the police, she'd had to discipline herself when it came to her feelings and emotions especially when dealing with the families of people who had been killed or murdered. It had become a habit that was hard to break. So here she was again, trying to muster as much self-control as she could, when all she really wanted to do was give in to her feelings and break down.

As she walked towards her car, searching blindly through her bag for the keys, a voice said "You can't fool me, even with those sunglasses."

She turned around, as she recognised the soft voice of her close friend.

"Oh Kathy!" she cried "Thanks for coming."

The woman put her arms around Josephine as she sobbed, for what seemed like an eternity. It was such a relief to be able to release all the emotions and sadness that had been pent up inside her for so long. When she finally recovered, Josephine opened her car door, and sat in the driver's seat. She looked in her rear-view mirror at her red swollen eyes, and the black streaks of mascara that had run down her cheeks.

"Oh my God! What a state! Do you think anyone will ever fancy me again?"

"I doubt it," her friend replied laughing.

"Kathy, have you come in your car?" Josephine asked as she wiped away the black streaks from her face.

"No, I caught a taxi."

"Well would you mind driving me home? Only the way I feel I might crash the car!"

"Of course, move over," Kathy replied. "But you're not going home. I'm taking you for a drink."

"Oh... I don't know..." Josephine started.

"Well I do, and I'm in charge!" Kathy replied.

* * *

Some thirty minutes or so later, Kathy was sitting by the window, in a charming little bistro restaurant in Torquay overlooking the sea. When Josephine emerged from the 'Ladies' she looked slightly more presentable after washing her face, and applying some fresh make-up, even though her eyes were still a little swollen. She was in her mid-forties with short blonde hair which had a few strands of grey, which were not really noticeable because they blended in with her own colour. Her deep blue-grey eyes had been her best feature in her youth, and they still retained a certain sparkle despite the fine lines beneath them.

Sitting down at the table, she noticed Kathy had ordered her a brandy. She cupped the glass in her hands and held it to her lips as she sipped the drink.

"I needed that, but I hope I don't turn to drink now Tom's gone," she said smiling at her friend.

"I don't suppose you'll be able to afford to, now you've taken out a mortgage extension to pay him off," Kathy replied.

Just then the waiter came over to the table with two omelettes, a bowl of chips and a mixed salad.

"I'm not hungry," Josephine said

"Eat it!" Kathy ordered her, as if she was talking to some naughty child.

"Okay Mum," she replied smiling.

Some time later, having cleared her plate, even though she had insisted she had no appetite, Josephine lit a cigarette as she stirred her coffee.

"I really didn't want to start smoking again," she began, "But it's the stress of the divorce."

"I know, you've done well, given up for two

years wasn't it?" Kathy asked.

"Yes, even when I had some bad cases at work to deal with, I was never tempted, and it's taken a man to get me back on this bad habit," she said a little bitterly.

"Don't be too hard on yourself Jo, he wasn't just any man, you had spent the last twenty years with him."

Kathy suddenly wished she hadn't mentioned Tom and her regret showed in her face. Josephine recognised this at once. They had been friends for many years, and could easily pick up any kind of trauma or upset the other was going through.

"It's not a taboo subject, you know, Kathy. Obviously people will still mention Tom," she reassured her.

"Do you think you made the right decision keeping the house on?"

"The mortgage we had was low – I could afford to re-mortgage on my salary and give Tom his half."

"The police force must pay well! What's the going rate for Detective Inspector nowadays?" Kathy joked. Josephine didn't answered.

"Don't you think the house is a bit big for you though, Jo?"

"Well, I suppose you're right, but I like it so much there at Babbacombe, and I've always loved the sea view. I don't know yet if Jessica will come home, or stay in Nottingham after she gets her degree."

She thought for a moment or so as she sipped her coffee.

"I know the place holds memories, and in time I may decide I need to sell up and move, but at this moment, it's a safe haven for me, and I can't imagine living anywhere else."

Chapter 3

TWO DAYS LATER Detective Inspector Josephine Blake returned to the station. She was a little apprehensive, wondering how her colleagues would act towards her. The last thing she wanted was to be treated with kid gloves, but at the same time she knew that the peoplc she worked with had liked Tom, and some had thought she was to blame for the breakdown in their marriage, despite the fact Tom was now living with another woman.

She walked through the main entrance. It was bustling with people and everybody seemed busy. The desk Sergeant looked up from the form he was completing for some woman who had lost her dog, and gave her a quick smile.

"Morning ma'am." Before she had even had chance to answer he had looked away and started talking to the woman.

She had been in her office about fifteen minutes or so, and was sifting through the paperwork on her desk. Everything seemed in order, and there wasn't much for her to do. Just at that moment Detective Sergeant Bill Hughes, poked his head round the door, "Busy?" he asked.

"No, I wish I was in fact," she replied.

He walked into the room and sat opposite her.

"Well I suppose you'll be on the look out now," he said.

"What do you mean?" she asked.

"For another man," he smirked.

"For God's sake Bill, I was only in court two days ago!"

"Well you can't let the grass grow under your feet, not at your age!"

"And I was worried you might think that I was feeling sensitive. I must have been mad!"

"I've been through it all myself, if you ever need a bit of help or advice," he said in a serious voice.

Josephine burst out laughing.

"Oh Bill, you're a case. You've really cheered me up!"

"Well at least I've been of *some* use then," he replied bitterly, as he left the office.

* * *

Some time later Detective Constable Sally James knocked on Josephine's door and entered. Josephine was in a pensive mood as she stared out of her window.

"Hello ma'am," she said briskly.

For a moment she startled her. "Oh I'm sorry… I was miles away… it's good to see you Sally."

The young DC was tempted to ask how she was feeling, but decided against it as she thought her DI would be fed up of people asking the same question.

"It's good to have you back ma'am," she said smiling. "I don't know whether the Sarge has mentioned it to you, but you're in court this Friday."

Josephine looked puzzled. DC James continued "It's concerning the manslaughter case, Doreen Miles."

"Of course I remember now, I knew I'd be called to give evidence, but she's been in prison awaiting the trial date for several weeks," Josephine said.

Some two months earlier in June, Doreen Miles had stabbed her husband Peter to death. According to her statement, he had been a brute and a bully for many years, and one of her children had been taken into care, because her father had abused her; also on several occasions Mrs Miles had been admitted to hospital with broken ribs and black eyes due to her husband's violence. She had put up with it for many years, until she could take no more and finally snapped.

Although Josephine could sympathise with the woman, she felt that Doreen Miles should have reported her husband's violence in the past so that criminal charges could have been brought against him, but she had suffered in silence for a long time. The lawyer representing Doreen Miles was Anthony Ryan, who Josephine had known for some time. He had advised her to plead guilty to manslaughter, and Josephine had agreed with him that it was the only option open to the woman. Despite the fact Ryan had a good reputation, and she knew him to be a good lawyer, Josephine feared the woman would still have to serve a few years in prison.

"Can you get me the case file Sally? I need to study it. By the way do we know who's presiding?"

"I think it's Judge Abraham."

Josephine thought for a moment and then said "I can recall giving evidence in a case before, when he was on the bench, some time last year I think it was, he's a bit of a stickler if I remember. I'll have to get my act together before I go into the witness box."

"I'm sure you'll be fine, ma'am," Sally assured her.

"Maybe in the past I'd have been more

confident, but I'm not so certain now."

"Well I am. You'll be able to handle Judge Abraham perfectly well."

"Thanks for having so much confidence in me, Sally," Josephine replied.

"We all have, but you just don't realise it ma'am… by the way can I get you a drink from the canteen?"

"I tell you what, I'll go down with you. I could do with seeing a few familiar faces."

As Sally waited at the counter, Josephine thought *'When she started here two years ago, she lacked confidence and was too nervous of the job, I often had to encourage her to say what she felt, and to stand up for herself, and now she's having to give me support! God I feel old! At least I've been successful with her, she's turned out a very confident young woman. I think it's time she applied for promotion, in fact perhaps it's time I retired.'*

As Josephine drank her tea, her mind was in turmoil.

* * *

"Retire! Don't talk ridiculous Mum, you're only forty four," Jessica's voice sounded at the other end of the phone.

"That's quite old in the police force. Anyway I thought you wanted me to spend more time with you?" she replied

"I did when I was younger, but now I'm away, and with Dad gone, whatever would you do with yourself all day?"

"I don't mean retire from working completely, just from the police. I could always do lectures or something… oh I don't know"

"Mum, you're a brilliant cop!"

Josephine hated it when Jessica used that word – it sounded so American.

"You've solved some really difficult cases in the past. I talk about you to all my friends… I'm so proud of you" .

Josephine felt touched and her voice faltered,. "You… er… never told me this before… I didn't know."

"That's because you never spoke of jacking it all in before… Anyway I'm coming home next week for a few days to do a dissertation and some revision. So we can have a picnic on Dartmoor," she suggested.

"God, we haven't done that for years, I used to love it up there, it's so peaceful and remote."

"It's a date then, start packing the hamper. See you next week then Mum." Jessica put down the receiver before Josephine had the chance to reply.

Josephine felt depressed as she walked into the kitchen. She plugged in the kettle and opened the fridge door, all that was in there was a few eggs and a piece of cheese. The sight of the fridge with its sparse contents made her sad, as she recalled when Tom and Jessica were at home, it used to be crammed full of food. It needed to be in those days, as Jessica's friends seemed to be like permanent lodgers. *'To think I used to moan about them and all the noise they made, at least the house was full of life, now it's like a morgue,'* she thought.

Just as she was resigning herself to a quiet night in, with a cheese omelette and a mug of tea, the phone rang.

"Hello," she answered lethargically.

"Josephine, it's Andrew Blythe here."

"Oh, hello."

"Are you okay, only you sounded odd when you answered the phone?"

"I'm fine," she said.

"Don't lie... I'm a psychologist, or had you forgotten? Even though I can't see your face, I can tell by your voice you're not."

"Okay clever dick, so I'm not exactly ecstatic. Tom's gone, Jessica's gone, and the house is so quiet you can hear a pin drop, and to top it all I'm about to have a fun filled evening with a cheese omelette in front of the box," she said sarcastically.

"That's just where you're wrong. I'm taking you out to dinner, say eight o'clock, that gives you half an hour, that's enough time isn't it?"

"Oh... well... I'm not really in the mood."

"Precisely, that's exactly why you're coming, just what the doctor ordered. See you at eight."

He hung up before she had the chance to object further to his offer. *'God, what the hell's wrong with me? I'm fed up, there's an offer of a date and I'm making excuses!'* she thought

She suddenly felt quite apprehensive. *'A date! I haven't had one of those in years, not since Tom and I were courting.'* She went upstairs and had a quick shower, and then put on her make-up. As she opened her wardrobe door, she noticed a stylish deep blue dress she had bought for a party some months earlier, but she hadn't worn it, as she'd backed out at the last minute. When she had first bought the dress it was a little tight, but with all the stress and worry of the divorce, Josephine had lost a few pounds in weight, and when she tried it on, it fitted like a glove. This cheered her up, and she became a little more enthusiastic about her date.

Andrew Blythe, the forensic psychologist, had been a friend of Josephine's for the past three years. He had always hoped that their relationship would become more than 'just good friends', especially when two years previously, Tom had moved out of the house for a few months. To Andrew's disappointment, Tom had returned, and he and Josephine had decided to both try harder and work at their marriage. Eventually things became impossible, and they drifted further apart, so when Tom had told her he was seeing someone else, they both decided the only option left open to them was divorce, although Josephine had no one special in her life.

It was five to eight; Josephine was almost ready, and was just putting her ear-rings on when the doorbell rang. She answered the door feeling a little nervous.

As Andrew stood at the door, she thought how attractive he looked. He was in his late forties, with dark hair that was greying slightly at the temples. His eyes were a pale icy blue, a feature he had inherited from his Norwegian mother, he looked tanned and fit due to a recent holiday he had just returned from, and his deep complexion made his eyes look even bluer. He wore a denim shirt, with a tie and a navy blazer.

"You look well," Josephine remarked.

"So do you," he replied as he looked her up and down. "I must admit," he sighed, "That dress... you look gorgeous."

"Can a middle-aged Detective Inspector look gorgeous?" she asked, as she laughed.

"Most definitely," he replied smiling like a Cheshire cat.

***

The restaurant was secluded and quiet.

"What do you fancy?" Andrew asked as he read the menu.

"I think I'll let you order, it's been ages since anyone made a decision for me," Josephine said playfully.

They started with celery soup, followed by lemon sole with fresh vegetables and a bottle of Chardonnay. When they had finished their meal, Andrew poured the remaining wine into their glasses, and he raised his to Josephine.

"This is to you and a new beginning,"

Josephine didn't touch her glass.

"I wish I could feel that way Andrew, but I feel it's like the end not the beginning. In fact, retirement had crossed my mind."

He didn't look shocked or surprised as he put his glass back down on the table.

"I can understand you feeling that way, with Jessica gone, and your divorce from Tom. I suppose you don't feel that you've much of a purpose in life at the moment, and the insecurity you're feeling has spilled over into your profession," he said sympathetically.

"You've summed it up in a nutshell," she replied.

"You don't need me to tell you that if you did decide to resign, it would be one of the worst decisions you could ever make. You're damn good at your job and I think you know that" .

"Maybe that was the problem. I was too good at my job, and not good enough as a wife and mother," she replied.

"I disagree, you've done a marvellous job bringing Jessica up, she's a fine young woman with a good head on her shoulders, and when she graduates I'm sure she'll do well, in whatever career she chooses. Has she got any ideas yet?" Andrew asked.

"The degree she's taking is business studies and finance, and I'm not sure what she'll do, but I'm proud of her."

"Anyway apart from Jessica... Okay, so things didn't work out for you and Tom in the end, but the marriage did last for over twenty years, so it was by no means a failure. You're still a very attractive woman – you've got a lot to offer any man Jo... and don't you forget it!"

She was thoughtful for a moment and then said "Thank you for asking me out tonight Andrew, it was just what I needed to get me out of this rut, and you're right, I do need to be more optimistic," she raised her glass to his. "Let's say, to me, working at a new beginning with a positive attitude."

"I'll drink to that," he said as their glasses chinked together.

"By the way I liked your choice of menu," she told Andrew.

"I like to cook at home, in fact I'm getting quite adventurous trying out new recipes, I'll have to cook for you one evening."

"I can remember when you were first divorced, you couldn't even boil an egg," Josephine reminded him.

"That's true, I left Frances to do everything, so when we split up I lived on junk food to start with. In fact I'd probably never have experienced the joy of cooking if we'd still have been married!"

"How long has it been now?" Josephine inquired.

"Five years, and as you know Luke had already left home by the time the divorce was settled, so that was one less complication."

"I thought you might re-marry, it wouldn't be too late to start another family."

"Are you offering?" he said laughing.

"No way! My child bearing days are over, even though I haven't been through the menopause yet."

The expression on Andrew's face suddenly turned serious. "Listen Jo... I don't want you to think I'm making a move on you, just because you're free! I feel that if we can just be good friends, I'm here for you, even if you just want to talk."

Since Andrew had asked Josephine out in the

past, even when she was still with Tom, she had thought that perhaps he was attracted to her, and despite the fact she wasn't ready to have a serious relationship with another man, she was a little dismayed he just wanted to be friends. She didn't let her disappointment show and replied "I didn't think for one moment you were making a move on me, and yes it would be nice to have a male friend, even though I've got lots of female ones."

He settled the bill and then drove her home. As his car pulled up outside the house, Josephine decided not to ask him in.

"It was a lovely evening Andrew, thank you."

As he went to kiss her, she turned her cheek towards him, but he cupped her face in his hands and turned it towards him, and covered her face and neck in kisses. Shc couldn't remember ever having such a passionate embrace. She felt alive for the first time in months; Josephine responded just as passionately and began to feel sexually aroused. She was just about to ask him in, when her pager started bleeping.

"Oh no! I don't believe this," she said noticing the number was her Sergeant, Bill Hughes'.

"What time is it?" she asked Andrew.

"One o'clock," Andrew replied a little breathless.

"I haven't got my mobile on me."

"Use mine," Andrew offered, as he reached for

his phone.

"No it's okay, I'll use the phone inside," she got out of his car a little dishevelled.

"I'll ring you next week," he said before driving off.

When Josephine finally found her key and let herself into the house, she flopped on the sofa. She felt exhausted *'God, I'd never have thought Andrew could be so passionate,'* she thought. *'Or me, for that matter'*

The sound of the phone ringing brought her back down to earth.

"Hello ma'am, Bill here. Is your pager working?"

"Yes Bill, I was just about to ring you."

"I've been trying your home phone – I couldn't reach you on your mobile."

"I think I must have turned it off. I've been out, and had a wonderful evening," she told him.

"Well I'm afraid I'm going to spoil it for you, we've found the body of a young woman. She's been stabbed several times – it's not a pretty sight... I'll give you the address."

"Bill, can you send a squad car to my house? Only I've had quite a lot of wine to drink tonight."

"Will do, there's one in the area, so I'll make sure it will be with you shortly. The adress is seventy three Hellaby Road."

"Right Bill, I'm on my way."

Josephine walked over to the mirror, her face was smeared with lipstick, and her hair was a mess. She had just enough time to wash her face and brush her hair, before the police car arrived. She quickly grabbed a long raincoat and slipped it on over her short blue dress.

Chapter 4

IT WAS NEARLY two in the morning, when the car pulled up outside seventy three Hellaby Road, which was a pre-war semi-detached house, and even though all the houses in the road were more or less the same, they did have a certain character with large, round bay windows with coloured stained glass in the top sections.

As Josephine entered the house, it was full of police officers and the forensic team, in their white suits and hoods. The house and garden had been cordoned off with tape, and one officer had commenced the log, and was taking the names of everyone as they arrived on the scene.

"DI Blake," Josephine told him, as she entered the hallway. It was dark and shabby, despite the fact that it was fitted with a vivid orange patterned carpet.

The design looked familiar to Josephine, and

then she remembered that her mother had had a similar one in her lounge in the sixties, which led Josephine to think someone middle-aged or elderly lived in the house, even though Bill had mentioned to her that the victim was a young woman.

Just as Josephine was about to go up, Bill walked down the stairs, wearing a white zip-up suit that the forensic team had given him. He looked pale and tense. He held another suit in his hand for Josephine to wear.

"Are you okay, Bill?" she asked.

Even though they had been at many rather nasty murder scenes in the past, they never seemed to affect Bill as much as they did Josephine. He hardly ever appeared shocked or upset, or if he did, he was a master at disguising his feelings.

Just as he was about to answer her, a PC came running down the stairs past Bill, nearly knocking him over; the PC's face looked green and he seemed terrified.

"Oh God!" he cried, as he ran out of the front door, and started retching on the lawn.

"What the hell's going on, Bill?"

"I think you'd better go into the lounge and put this on before we go up," Bill suggested. Josephine took the suit from him and went into the room. Despite his shocked state, Bill was surprised when Josephine removed her raincoat, to reveal a rather sexy short blue dress.

"Been to a party?" he asked.

"No, just a date with a friend," she replied stepping into the suit with some difficulty. As she pulled up the zip she said "Right, can we go up Bill? We've wasted enough time as it is, don't you think?"

"It's not a pretty sight," he said.

"When is it any different?"

"The police surgeon has certified death, and he's contacted the pathologist Brian Morrison. He's here now. A maniac's been at work up there ma'am, I've seen some sights in my time, but nothing like this," Bill said shakily.

'It must be worse than I imagined,' Josephine thought to herself. She took a deep breath and tried to take control of herself, as she made her way upstairs.

As she entered the crowded bedroom, she couldn't see the woman's body at first, just a large brass bedstead, and Brian Morrison's back, as he was bending over the bed. As he turned to look at her he didn't speak, which was unusual, as they were friends as well as colleagues. He moved to one side so Josephine could have a clear view of the body.

She was horrified as she took in the scene before her. It was far worse than any gruesome horror film. The victim's naked body was a mass of blood, most of it had dried to a sickly brown colour, but some was still bright crimson, and the stench was awful. Two sweeping incisions ran the width of the young woman's neck and had all but severed her head. Her chest had been hacked open and slashed many times.

Josephine felt almost paralysed with shock and horror and could hardly speak, as she asked quietly, "How long has she been dead?"

"It's difficult to say at the moment, but possibly at least two days, as most of the blood is not fresh as you can see."

Josephine started to sweat profusely. His voice seemed distant, as he continued to talk.

'I mustn't faint' she thought. Morrison noticed her swaying, and quickly took her by the arm, and sat her down on a chair.

"Are you alright?" he asked.

After a few moments, she started to recover.

"I'll be fine in a minute or two," she answered feebly.

"Just take deep breaths."

When she felt able, she stood up and said "I need to get some fresh air, I'll speak to you later."

She made her way downstairs and out into the front garden. It was a clear night with a full moon, and the air was fresh. Josephine took a few deep breaths, and feeling a little calmer she lit a cigarette. She was disappointed that she hadn't mustered enough will power and self control to have coped with the situation better. She walked a few yards further, taking in the cool night air, when she suddenly noticed that the young PC that had run out of the house earlier, was still being sick, and she thought that she hadn't handled herself quite so badly after all!

After a few minutes she went back into the house, where Bill Hughes was in the front lounge.

"Are you feeling better now?" he asked.

"I think so," she replied vaguely.

"I mean all that blood and those injuries, it's enough to make anyone..."

"I did see all the gruesome injuries, you know Bill, there's no need to elaborate!"

"Oh yes of course, sorry I..."

Josephine interrupted him before he had time to finish.

"Now what information do we have about the victim?"

Bill got out his pad and started to read.

"Her name is Jane Fielding, aged thirty-two, she lived here alone, and was unemployed."

"Who found the body?"

"The next door neighbour, a Mrs Kennedy. She suffers from angina and she collapsed when she found her. She is in the hospital at present."

"I'm not surprised, a scene like that's enough

to send anyone into a state of shock, let alone someone who has a heart complaint. The poor woman, it's a wonder it didn't kill her."

"We must be dealing with a bloody butcher. He's a *maniac*, I thought I had seen some sights in my time… but this! If I could get my hands on the sick bastard…" Bill said as his face started to turn red.

"Okay Bill, we're all uptight, but let's get back to the facts. So who called the police?"

"It was the husband, Mr Kennedy."

"Right, we'll speak to him later this morning, there's no point waking him now," she looked at her watch. It was nearly three in the morning.

After he had examined the body as much as he could at the scene, Morrison instructed the forensic team to cover the victim's face and hands with plastics bags to keep any fibres or skin that might be found on them intact, for when more extensive tests were carried out on them back at the forensic laboratory. The victim was then placed into the black zip-up body bag, and carefully carried down the stairs.

"Right then, I want the entire house and garden cordoned off, and a PC left on duty outside to stop anyone from entering. In a few hours I want us to start interviewing the neighbours," Josephine instructed the team, who were now downstairs.

Just as she'd finished speaking, Brian Morrison entered the lounge.

"I'm sorry I had to leave the room," she apologised to him.

"Don't worry, we even had one PC pass out, and to be honest even I felt a little queasy," he admitted.

"Yet you have to dissect bodies all day, I'd have thought you would have been unaffected," Josephine replied.

"Well that's true," Morrison said as he wiped his sweaty brow. "But we do it deftly, so the body doesn't look bad for the victims' families when they come to view their loved ones. This is just butchery!"

Morrison looked tired and taut. He was in his early thirties and married with a young family. Josephine had worked with him on many past cases, and she admired him. He was good at his job, but also caring and sensitive, especially when dealing with the families of the deceased.

"Can you tell me anything now?" she asked.

"I can't be certain, until further, more extensive tests are carried out on the body, but I'm pretty certain that she was strangled before her neck and body were slashed, as I found marks and bruises on her neck when I removed some of the congealed blood. I suspect she may already have been dead before he started to cut her. Anyway,

I'll go home for a couple of hours for a rest, as I'll be working on the body all day, although I doubt I'll be able to sleep!"

"I don't think any of us will," Josephine added.

"I'll give this case priority. I can pass my other cases over to a colleague, and if I work around the clock it's possible that I might have some information for you by tomorrow at the latest, I hope."

"That's fine, I'll speak to you then," Josephine replied. She then turned to two officers and told them to initiate house to house enquiries later that morning, before she went outside.

By this time, a crowd of people had gathered on the road, despite the unearthly hour and the cold, they seemed determined not to miss anything.

"Look at this lot!" Bill remarked.

"It's only what we can expect, it's human nature to be curious," Josephine replied.

Bill turned to look at the scene of police activity, the chequered capped officers, the blue flashing lights and the blue and white tape being put around the fence of the garden of the murder house.

Just as Josephine was walking to the car she was recognised by two of the press men. They came running towards her and literally pleaded with her for the briefest of interviews, or even a one line statement.

"Oh come on, Detective Inspector Blake, can't you give us anything?" one asked, blocking the car door.

"Please get out of my way, I'll be giving a statement later today when I have more details."

"But I only wanted..." Before he had chance to finish DS Bill Hughes pushed past him and opened the car door for Josephine.

"You heard what she said, you'll have to wait till later. Now move away from the car please." They both got in and drove off.

* * *

"Thanks. You handled that very well Sergeant. I mean you didn't even swear, and you said please. It's so unlike you, keeping your temper with the press," she said a little sarcastically.

"Well, if you must know, I wouldn't like to tell you what I felt like saying. I noticed one of the film crew and I thought they'd have a field day if they caught me losing my rag," he said, slightly angry in defence.

"I'm glad you handled it, Bill. I didn't even see the camera, with all the flashing lights," she replied.

As they were driving away, Josephine said, "I don't think there's any point going to bed, I won't sleep."

"I know what you mean. I'm wide awake, and funny enough I'm famished, even though I felt sick earlier on," Bill replied.

"It's nervous tension, it causes your blood sugar level to drop. I'm hungry even though I've had a meal," she looked at her watch, "God, that was over eight hours ago. I'll tell you what, come back to mine and I'll cook breakfast, then we can go into the station at about seven."

"That's fine by me," Bill replied.

After they had arrived at Josephine's house, she put on a pot of strong coffee.

"That'll keep us alert," she said.

"Mmm, I just fancy a fry up," Bill said.

"Oh! I've just thought, I've only got eggs in the fridge. I'm sorry to disappoint you, but it will have to be omelettes I'm afraid."

Josephine made two large omelettes with a box of six eggs, with added cheese and dried herbs. They turned out to be quite tasty and filling. After they had finished eating, they drank coffee and smoked.

"It's ironic," Josephine began, "Nothing much was happening when I returned to work after the divorce, and I wanted some absorbing case to take my mind off it, and now we've got one, I don't think I can cope."

"You always cope," Bill told her, as he lifted

the percolator and poured himself another coffee.

"I wish I had the confidence in myself, that everyone else seems to have," she sighed.

"Anyway who did you go out for a meal with?"

"I don't think that's any of your business," she replied teasingly.

Bill felt tired and was unable to tell if Josephine was teasing him, or really didn't want to give out any details about her date.

"That's rich! I can remember telling you all about *my* dates, when Mary and I split up," he said.

"That's only because you decided to broadcast it all over the station."

"Well, you *were* giving me tips on what to wear, and where to take the ladies in question, so don't say you weren't interested."

"Okay Bill, I admit maybe I did give advice that wasn't needed. Perhaps you shouldn't have listened to me – I'm not exactly successful when it comes to the marriage stakes, now am I? How *is* Joyce, anyway?" she asked.

Bill had been dating Joyce for the past six months. She was divorced with teenage children. He was reluctant to tell Josephine what was happening in his love life on this occasion, because she was being so secretive about her own private life, but he loved to talk and would always discuss things, unlike most men. He couldn't resist confiding in her.

"I moved in for a week or two," he began "But I just couldn't handle her family. The lad's nineteen and the daughter's sixteen."

"Oh, they can be very rebellious at that age," she intervened.

"You're telling me! I couldn't stand the rows and the shouting, so I moved back home to my flat. Don't get me wrong, I'm still very fond of Joyce, and we see each other about twice a week, sometimes she stops with me, but there's no way I could take on a family."

"That's understandable. Even though you and Mary never had any children, I don't think it would have made much difference if you had. You put up with more from your own kids than you do other people's and believe me teenagers are a pain to cope with no matter how much past experience you've had. You know how it has been with Jessica," Josephine replied, as she thought back on all the trials and tribulations she had had with her daughter during her teenage years.

"Anyway," Bill continued, "It suits me now I've moved back to my own place, and they may leave home eventually, and maybe then I'll move back in with Joyce."

"Don't count on it Bill," Josephine joked, "They most probably know which side their bread's buttered!"

"Anyway I've rattled on long enough, and it's obvious that you're not going to tell me anything about your date," Bill grunted.

"Let's just say that I was out with a friend," Josephine replied, bringing the conversation to an end.

Even though they were both exhausted, Josephine knew that she wouldn't sleep, so she went upstairs to shower, and then she changed into a navy suit and a white shirt-style blouse.

As she walked into the lounge, Bill was standing by the window smoking, looking out to sea.

"Fabulous, this view," he stated without turning round, "I can see why you didn't want to sell up."

"You're the only one who can then," she replied, walking over to her desk. She picked up her briefcase and bag. "Ready to go then?"

Bill turned around and stubbed out his cigarette in a nearby ashtray. He looked up at his DI.

"I'll tell you one thing, ma'am," he said.

"What's that?" Josephine asked.

"I much prefer the dress you wore last night!"

Chapter 5

THEY ARRIVED AT THE STATION at about seven-thirty a.m., although there wasn't a lot they could get on with. Josephine had instructed a group of police officers to call at all the houses in Hellaby Road and speak to the residents, from eight-thirty onwards, so she didn't expect any relevant information until at least midday.

It was nine-fifteen when DC Roger Barnes entered the incident room. By that time Josephine had tied up any loose ends of previous cases, and completed all of her paperwork, which she loathed doing as she found it a real chore. At the same time she felt relieved she had managed to get it all done, as she knew she'd have no spare time now, with this murder case to work on.

"Did you find out about Jane Fielding's next of kin?" she asked Barnes.

"Yes ma'am, there's a brother, Peter Fielding,

he lives in Swindon, we've contacted him and he's on his way down to us. He should be here about lunch time."

"Right, I think we'll go and see the next door neighbour," she flicked though her pad for a moment, "Here we are, Mr Kennedy, at number seventy-five, and then afterwards if she is well enough for visitors we'll go to the hospital and speak to his wife, who found the body, although I regret having to put her though the ordeal of having to remember such a gruesome scene."

"I don't suppose she'll ever forget it!" remarked Bill.

"No... I don't think she will," Josephine agreed as she thought about the terrible scene she had encountered some hours earlier.

* * *

Josephine and Bill parked their car at the end of the road, as there were still two police cars outside the victim's house. They were relieved to find that no press or TV crews were about as they approached the house. Police Sergeant Thomas walked towards them, as they reached the gate and opened it.

"Morning ma'am," he said.

"It's okay Sergeant, we're going next door to speak to the neighbour."

"Alright ma'am."

"By the way, what's happened to all the media?" Bill asked.

"I managed to get rid of them," he replied a little proudly.

"Well done, Thomas," Josephine said, as she walked down the path of the adjoining semi.

The door was opened after a moment or so, by a white-haired man who looked to be in his late sixties. Despite his age he looked fit and tanned. They showed their warrant cards as they introduced themselves.

"Oh... yes... you'd better come in." He showed them into the back lounge which overlooked the garden.

"I don't suppose you got much sleep last night with all the police activity and the crowds outside," Bill said.

"You're telling me! This is usually such a quiet road. I've never seen so many people. I thought it was hectic when we had a street party in nineteen-seventy-seven, when we celebrated the Queen's Jubilee but this..."

"I believe that you've lived here for some time?" Bill stated.

"Nearly thirty years," he replied.

"How's Mrs Kennedy?" Josephine enquired.

"I'm relieved to say, she's okay now, but I was worried about her, I can tell you, I saw poor Jane myself and it was awful... just awful, and what with Elsie suffering from angina, I just thank the Lord the attack wasn't fatal, although it's the worst that she has ever had."

"I'm not surprised," Bill commented. "I'd like you to tell us all that you can about Jane, and also the events leading up to your wife finding the body. It may take some time."

"Don't worry, I've got plenty of that now that I am retired, not that I don't keep myself active you know."

"I can see that, you look very fit for your age, Mr Kennedy," Josephine commented.

"I do my best," he replied glancing at the clock on the mantelpiece. It was ten-forty.

"Do you have to go to Torbay hospital to visit your wife this morning?" Josephine asked.

"Our daughter's going this morning, so I said that I'd visit her this afternoon, about two o'clock. So I've plenty of time, but I'll make us some tea before we start, if that's okay?"

"That will be fine," Josephine replied smiling.

After they had finished their tea, Bill got out his pen and his pad to take notes.

"I take it Jane Fielding lived alone in the house?" Josephine started.

"Well yes, for the past six months or so," Mr Kennedy answered.

"So did she have a partner, or a lodger who

lived there before?"

"Oh, goodness no. She looked after her mother who'd been ill for quite some time. It was her parents' house originally."

Josephine recalled her first impression of the house. She had thought that the furnishings were quite old fashioned for a young woman, but now the reason for this was clear, the choice of furnishings was that of her parents and they had never been changed.

"Joe and Winnie Fielding moved in next door, a couple of years before Elsie and I bought our house. They were a little older than us. I think Winnie was seventy-two when she died. She didn't have Jane until she was nearly forty. Peter was born ten years earlier."

"Of course, that's the brother. He's travelling down from Swindon today, so we'll be speaking to him later."

Mr Kennedy continued to reminisce. "Joe died about, let me think, nineteen-ninety-three, I think it was, it was about five years ago, and yet it doesn't seem that long. Still, at my age time flies."

"It does at any age," Bill added.

"So did Jane move back in with her Mum?" Josephine asked Mr Kennedy.

"She never left. That's been her home from the day she was born."

"So, Jane must have been about thirty-two

then... any steady boyfriends on the scene?" Bill asked.

"I've seen one or two lads come and go over the years. She wasn't a bad looking girl."

Josephine's mind suddenly flashed back to the crime scene as she tried to remember the victim's face, but it was difficult to see amidst all of the blood.

"I don't suppose you've a recent photo?" she asked.

"I'm afraid I don't, though I think Jane had some photos taken with her mother just before she died. They should be in the house somewhere. Jane always kept a family album."

"We haven't checked her belongings yet, but we'll look into that when we do," Josephine added.

"So you say she had the odd boyfriend, but no-one special?"

"There was one young man, he used to call at the house, quite a lot if I remember, but that was about a year ago, but as Winnie's condition deteriorated, cancer you know, Jane had to stay in and nurse her mother around the clock, and I don't think she saw the young man again, or any other men for that matter."

"Did she go to work?" Bill asked.

"She used to work in some offices in town, filing clerk, or something like that. Elsie would probably know the address, but she gave her job up. I'm sure that she hasn't worked for at least a year."

"I wonder how she managed financially?" Bill said.

"Well, the house was paid for. There's no mortgage, and I'm sure that Winnie and Joe had some savings. I can remember them being very prudent, almost mean, to tell you the truth. Winnie had Joe's life insured and I think she had a nice little windfall when he died, not that that's any compensation when you have lost someone you loved, you understand. Come to think of it, I'm sure Jane said something about getting a care allowance for looking after her mother from Social Services."

"Still, it couldn't have been much of a life for a young woman," Josephine commented.

"I know. She didn't go out much at all when her mother was alive, although from time to time, Elsie and I would sit with Winnie if Jane went to the cinema, but she was never away for long. We offered several times to let Jane have a break but she was always very reluctant to leave Winnie."

"Didn't the brother ever help out?" Josephine asked.

"He visited occasionally, and brought his wife and children with him. I suppose he was very busy and didn't really have much time."

"So all of the responsibility fell on Jane's

shoulder's to look after her terminally ill mother," Josephine stated.

"Yes, you're right. She didn't have much of a life, but she's made up for it since. She'd been going out a lot recently."

"I suppose she was making up for lost time," Bill suggested.

"Have you seen anyone come to the house recently, Mr Kennedy?" Josephine asked.

"No, I can't say that I have. I don't know whether Elsie would have done, but I doubt it."

"No girlfriends either?" Bill suggested. Mr Kennedy thought for a moment or so, and then said, "Jane was always a bit of a loner. If she did make any friends after her Mum died, I'm sure that she never brought them back to the house."

"Right. That seems to be all on that score, for the time being anyway, but if you do remember anything that may be relevant, please do not hesitate to contact me."

"I will definitely, and my wife may be able to tell you more, if there is anything I've missed, when she is better."

"Now I just need to ask you how it came about… finding the body. Although I know that it will be unpleasant for you going over the details," Josephine said gently.

"Jane gave Elsie a spare front door key, in case she ever lost her own. Anyway, Elsie became concerned when she noticed that the milk hadn't been taken in for a day or so. We got on well with Jane, and we knew that she'd always let us know if she was going away for a couple of days. She'd call in at least twice a week for a cup of tea and a chat, so we thought it was odd that we hadn't seen her. We tried phoning a couple of times but there was no reply."

"Can you remember the last time that you saw her alive?" Bill asked.

"Let me think. What day is it today?"

"Monday."

"Oh! Of course. What with Elsie being in hospital and poor Jane, I've got forgetful." He sounded embarrassed. "I think it was last Friday." He was quiet and thoughtful for a few moments and then said, "Yes, I remember, I was mowing the front lawn, and she came out and said that she was going to the shops."

"So let's see. That was Friday the thirtieth of August. So when did you and Mrs Kennedy become concerned?" Josephine asked.

"I can remember seeing the lights on in the house on Friday evening. She didn't bring in her milk on Saturday morning, but we just thought that she must be having a lie in. Then on Sunday we saw the Sunday paper still in the door, and another pint of milk left. I suggested to Elsie that she may have gone to stay at her brother's house for a couple of days, but Elsie was adamant that Jane wouldn't go away without letting us know. Anyway, Elsie was agitated all day on Sunday. She knocked on the door a few times and also tried phoning, but got no answer. I told her that all this worrying wasn't doing her angina any good. On Sunday evening, we had just finished watching the news, and I said that I'd make us some supper. Elsie said okay, but that she was going to get the key and go next door first. She thought that perhaps Jane was ill, or that possibly she had had a fall."

"So she went next door alone then?" Bill asked.

"Yes, I'm afraid she did," Mr Kennedy looked slightly guilty. "I said that I'd make us a sandwich and a drink while she was gone. If I'd have had even the slightest idea something was wrong, I'd never have let her go in there alone."

"Of course you wouldn't," Josephine reassured him. "You couldn't possibly have known what your wife was going to see."

"So what happened?" Bill asked.

"Well, she had been gone for about twenty minutes or so. I'd made us a sandwich and the pot of tea was going cold. To start with I wasn't unduly worried, as I thought that Jane was at home, and that they were just chatting. I just assumed that if no-one was in Elsie would have come straight home. Anyway a further fifteen minutes passed and I began to become anxious, so I went round there. The front door was slightly open so I walked into the hallway and shouted to Elsie. I looked in the lounge and the kitchen to begin with, and then when I came back into the hallway I heard a groaning noise coming from upstairs. I ran up to find Elsie lying on the landing. She couldn't speak and was making a dreadful moaning noise, and gasping for breath as she pointed to the bedroom."

"Did you go straight in there?" Josephine asked.

"Not to start with. I sat Elsie up with her back against the wall to help her breathing and then ran back home to get her tablets and spray. After she had taken her medication she seemed to recover slightly but she still couldn't speak. The doctor has since told me that was probably due to the shock, and not the angina attack. When I did go into Jane's room..." His faced looked drained and his voice faltered.

"Well, you know the rest... the poor girl. It was like something out of a horror film. I couldn't stay in the room as I felt sick and faint, but I knew I had to take hold of myself for Elsie's sake. I came back onto the landing. By this time Elsie could speak a little. I told her that I'd phone for an ambulance, and I told her to stay sitting, but she grabbed my arm and pleaded with me not to leave her. I could understand why she wanted to get back downstairs and out of the house, but I was worried that if I moved her she'd have another attack. Anyway I managed to get her down the stairs. I don't know how, she was so weak, like a dead weight. As soon as I got her back home she collapsed again and lost consciousness." His eyes filled with tears and he started to tremble.

Josephine touched his hand. "It must have been a terrible ordeal for you. I doubt that anyone could have done more in the circumstances."

"I suppose you're right," he said feeling in his trouser pocket for his handkerchief. He wiped his eyes and said, "Well that's about it. I phoned for an ambulance and for the police, but I couldn't go back into the house to see Jane. If only we had gone in earlier. Maybe we could have saved her."

"We think she may have been dead for at least two days when you discovered the body, but we can't be certain until we get the forensic report," Bill told him.

"I don't suppose that you heard any noises coming from next door? Only we think that there must have been some kind of struggle."

"No, funnily enough we didn't hear a thing. Mind you these houses are pre-war semi's and they're really well built. We've never really heard much noise coming from next door as the walls are so thick."

"Yes, they do look solidly built, not like the rubbish that's going up nowadays. The walls are so thin. A friend of mine has just moved onto a new estate, and he says that you can even hear next door's television and washing machine. It's a nightmare," Bill told him.

Josephine stood up. "Thank you for your time Mr Kennedy. You've been really helpful."

"Oh please. Call me George."

"We may need to speak to you again, and we'll also need to speak to your wife, when she is well enough, although she may not be able to tell us anything more than you have."

"I don't mind telling you, it's put the wind up us both. All those bloody maniacs out there these days."

"Just make sure that you keep all of your doors and windows shut. Although I don't think that you or your wife are in any danger, the chances of the murderer returning are so slim, but there will be one of our officers on duty next door if you're worried about anything."

"To be honest, Elsie and I don't feel like stopping in the house any longer," he said as he shut the front door.

As they drove back Josephine said to Bill, "That's today's society for you. They've lived in that house for thirty years and now they no longer feel safe there. It's so sad."

"And we don't know yet whether it was just some maniac prowling about or if Jane Fielding knew her murderer," Bill added.

"The SOCO's didn't find any signs of forced entry when they examined the doors and windows, so it points to her letting him in. I suppose he could have masqueraded as a salesman, but it's too soon to speculate. I'll have to contact Brian Morrison and see what information he has for me," Josephine told Bill.

When they got back to the station PC Sally James told them that Brian Morrison had been trying to contact them, as he had finished his post-mortem of Jane Fielding.

"Has the brother arrived yet?" Josephine asked her.

"No, not yet ma'am."

"Well, when he does, look after him for me Sally. Get him something from the canteen, and I'll be back as soon as I can."

"Will do, ma'am," Sally replied.

"Oh, and phone Brian Morrison and tell him that we are on our way."

"Can't we get something from the canteen before we go?" Bill asked.

"No. You know that you'll only feel queasy when you see the body. Let's get this over with first and then you can eat afterwards," Josephine replied.

"I don't think that I can hold out that long."

"You had that omelette that I cooked for you this morning," Josephine said as she mooched through her handbag. She produced a small packet containing three biscuits which she had managed to salvage from the bottom of the bag. "Here, these will tide you over," she said, as she threw the biscuits over to Bill.

Chapter 6

THEY STOOD IN the outer room and put on caps and gowns. Brian Morrison's assistant, a young man in his twenties, came into the room.

"I'm not looking forward to this," Josephine told him.

"The body isn't such a mess, now she's been cleaned up. You can just see the deep cuts on the body."

"Well, lead the way then, young man," Bill said, and they followed him in.

Morrison came over to them before they had reached where the victim lay.

"You look tired," Josephine said, noticing the dark circles beneath his eyes.

"I've been working on her from five-thirty this morning, although James here has kept me going with endless cups of coffee," he told them as he looked over at his young assistant. "He's only been with us for a week, and this is one of the worst cases I've ever seen; I think he's coped very well." The young man looked proud and obviously pleased with the praise, but he didn't say anything.

Brian Morrison pulled back the sheet that was covering Jane Fielding's body.

"The body had attracted a lot of fibres due to the amount of blood lost, so I've taped it all over, and have sent them to the lab. So they might have some information for us, when they have completed their tests. Now before I go into details about the stab wounds, which you can see are considerable, I want you to look at this," he lifted her arm and pointed to the wrist. "As you can see, there are pressure marks on both wrists; I originally thought she had been tied up, but on closer inspection I noticed these more severe marks, which I suspect have been made by handcuffs. These deep lines were made by the edges, they may have been used to shackle her to the brass bedstead. If fibres are found on her wrists it may have been that she was tied with a rope or cord of some sort, but I think it's doubtful."

"Could that indicate her assailant worked in security or the police?" the young man asked.

"Not necessarily," Bill began, "Handcuffs can now be purchased from sex shops and also can be ordered by mail order from certain combat magazines, it would be easy for anyone to get hold of a pair."

"I did find semen in the vagina."

"So was she raped before he murdered her?" Josephine asked.

"I don't think she was, there were no injuries to the walls of the vagina, to suggest forced entry; I think she actually consented to sex. So perhaps she knew him or at least trusted him. If she did ask him into her home, and agree to have sex with him, obviously she thought she was safe with him," Morrison continued with his findings. "Look here," he pointed to the cuts on the right side of her face, "Her face was also cut. The stab wounds on her chest were inflicted in rapid succession, and with much force – you can see the hilt marks on her chest. But this is what I found odd." He pointed to her arm, "The cuts to the right arm and hand suggest she was attempting to defend herself against the slashing of a wide sharp blade."

"I can't see what you're getting at," Josephine said.

"Although she was originally tied up, or shackled with handcuffs, he may have freed her right hand so she could defend herself."

"Why do that?" Bill inquired.

"I'm not expert in forensic psychology, as you know, but I've seen enough murder cases in my time, to know some people get more of a thrill out of killing, when they see their victims attempting to fight back, in a desperate attempt to cling onto life. What also leads me to think this happened is that these marks on her neck, where he exerted pressure, and some of the bruising, are not severe. I think he started to strangle his victim, but possibly didn't put enough pressure on the neck to kill her, maybe just enough for her to choke and feel faint, so she couldn't put up much of a fight. There were traces of blood and skin beneath her nails, which I think are from the assailant as she scratched him. I got that tested at the lab this morning and the blood group is A positive, whereas her blood group is O, so that more or less confirms my theory."

"Jesus, it sounds like wc'rc dealing with a sadistic butcher, who derives sheer pleasure and satisfaction in watching his victim's hopeless attempt as she fights for her life. What hell this poor girl must have gone through, and what terrible pain she endured. At least she's at peace now," Josephine said with tears in her eyes.

"So what do you think the actual cause of death was?" Bill asked.

"I'd say strangulation, and then when she was dead he cut her throat; he then inflicted further injuries. Her left lung was punctured and there was a stab wound to the heart."

"Have we got a time of death?" Josephine asked.

"When I examined the body, it was about one a.m. on Monday morning. I'd say she had been dead approximately forty-eight hours; the fact that the blood had congealed in places, also led me to think this time was fairly accurate."

"So let's think, she probably died in the early hours of Saturday morning, the thirty-first of August," Josephine added

"It could be a few hours either way, I think it's safe to assume death could have occurred say anytime between eleven p.m. on Friday night, and say four o'clock Saturday morning. Tests on the stomach contents, and her blood, showed she had consumed a fair amount of alcohol before she died."

"So it's possible she may have been drinking with her murderer," Josephine observed.

"He must have been covered in blood himself, and possibly it dripped through the house from his clothes, when he left," Morrison added.

"We haven't got the report back from the forensic lab yet, but there was a lot of blood all over the place," Bill said.

As Brian Morrison covered her body with the sheet, he turned to his assistant.

"Can I leave you to put the body away?"

"Yes of course, sir," he replied.

"Let's go into my office," Morrison said to Josephine and Bill. He could see they were both a little shaken by the results of the post-mortem, despite the fact they were both present at the scene of the crime.

"The only thing to add is that her general health was good, she had never had any children, but there was a small fibroid in the wall of her uterus. These are quite common in most women."

"Going back to the semen that you found. I think that she may have met her murderer in a pub, or that perhaps she had known him for some time. She'd invited him back and then after sex he had turned nasty," Bill suggested.

"Turned into a bloody monster, more like!" Josephine added.

"Well, thanks a lot Brian, at least we've got something to go on, but to be honest I don't relish the idea of parting with this information to the press, they'll have a field day. I can just see the headlines now. MANIAC KNIFE MAN LOOSE IN TORBAY!"

"They've been hanging around all morning, waiting for a statement from me on my findings, but luckily security managed to get rid of them about an hour ago," Brian told them.

"I know it's difficult, but when you do give them a statement, can you play it down a little? You know what it's like when the public start to panic," Josephine asked him.

"I'll just say that she was brutally murdered, and that the cause of death was strangulation. I won't give any of the sordid details if I can help it."

"Thanks a lot," Josephine said.

"If I find anything else I'll let you know, but at the moment all I need is sleep," he told them.

Bill who hardly ever displayed affection or physical contact, patted him on the back.

"You do that Brian, you need a good rest after what you've been through. It beats me how you can work on those bodies like you do."

"Oh... yes... thanks Bill," he replied in amazement.

"I forgot to mention that her brother is coming down from Swindon to identify the body, but I'll need to speak to him at the station first, so it may be late afternoon before one of our officers can bring him down," Josephine told him.

"It's always worse for the loved ones to have to see the body here rather than in the chapel of rest, so I'll personally see that her face and hair are done. Unless he insists, we won't uncover the body for him to see the injuries. We can't put a dress on her in case it disturbs any further evidence, as there's always the possibility we may have missed something, no matter how thorough we think we have been."

"I know that you'll do your best," Josephine said.

* * *

When they arrived back at the station, Peter Fielding had been there for about half an hour. DC Sally James had asked him to wait in one of the interview rooms, and had taken him coffee and sandwiches. As Josephine went into the room where Peter was waiting, Bill made his way to the canteen in the hope of getting whatever was left for his lunch.

"I'm sorry to have kept you waiting, Mr Fielding. I'm Detective Inspector Josephine Blake," she said as she shook his hand, "I hope my DC has been taking care of you."

"Yes, she brought me something to eat, but I'm afraid that I wasn't really hungry."

Josephine noticed the empty cup on the table and the unopened ham sandwich beside it.

"That's understandable. I'm so sorry about your sister."

Peter Fielding put his head in his hands and didn't reply. He was in his forties with dark hair like his sister, and seemed a plain, yet pleasant man. After a few moments he looked up. His eyes were red and tired.

"Poor Sis. She didn't have much of a life you

know, especially this last year as she had to look after our mother. I couldn't really help out much, with the family, although I did try to get down once a month with Julie and the children."

"How old are they?" asked Josephine.

"Anna's two and Luke's five," he replied.

"They're a handful at that age."

"You're telling me, but Jane loved to see them. When Mum was alive, Julie and I would sit in with her to give Jane a break, but she always insisted on taking the children down to the beach. We felt that she wasn't getting a break, but she said that she enjoyed taking them."

"I gather from your sister's neighbour Mr Kennedy, that Jane had always lived at home."

"Yes, that's right. They're good people, Elsie and George. I used to go to school with their son. I heard that poor Elsie found Jane's body and that it was a bit of a mess."

Josephine didn't reply, as she hadn't the heart to tell him the gruesome details at that moment.

He continued, "When Mum died she left the house to Jane. She suggested selling it and giving me half, but I refused. I told her that she had looked after them and that she deserved it."

"How long ago did you leave home, Mr Fielding?"

"Let me see. I think it was about seven years ago. After Mum died I told Jane to go out more and see a bit more of life, as I felt she'd missed out on so much. She lost touch with a lot of her friends when she gave up her job to nurse Mum. But I must admit that lately, I actually think that she took my advice. She'd always had a lovely slim figure, but used to wear old clothes. I know that she had splashed out on a couple of new outfits as she had showed them Julie the last time we visited. I think that she had started to go to pubs and clubs now and again, and I was pleased about this as she was still young and I'd hoped that she'd eventually meet someone and settle down."

"Did she have a boyfriend, do you know?" Josephine asked.

"I don't think so, I know that she'd always joke that she was 'playing the field', and just when she is finally having a life of her own this happens. It's dreadful. I can't believe it. Did he break in? Was it a burglar?"

"I'm afraid that it's too soon to tell, as we have only just started our investigations, but there were no signs of a break in. We think that she may have known her murderer. Or that she had at least let him in herself."

Peter Fielding looked confused and shaken as Josephine continued.

"Do you know of anyone who may want to kill your sister?" she asked.

"No... I mean surely... the idea's ludicrous. Everyone loved Jane."

"You didn't see her that often, there may have been things about her life you didn't know about," Josephine suggested.

"Well yes, you could be right, but we've always been close, even when we were younger; I'm sure if there was anything she was worried about, or anyone she was wary of, she'd have told me."

"Well if you can think of anything, please ring me," Josephine said as she handed him the card with her telephone number on. She stood up, "If you would like to view your sister's body now, for identification, one of my officers will drive you to the morgue."

"When can we start to arrange the funeral?" he asked.

"Not at the moment, I'm afraid. We can't release the body until we have carried out further forensic examinations."

As he stood up his face turned from grief and sadness to anger.

"Please tell me exactly how Jane died, Inspector."

"She was strangled, and her throat was cut I'm afraid," Josephine said, as gently as she could.

"Well then, for God's sake find the bastard who did this, because if I get my hands on him, you'll have another murder on your hands!"

* * *

When Josephine and Bill entered number seventy-three Hellaby Road, Josephine felt she had stepped back in time.

The pre-war semi consisted of three rooms downstairs, a lounge, dining room and kitchen. It was quite popular with this type of house to knock down the dividing wall, and make one large room, with a window at either end. But this house had kept its original character. The surfaces were still dusted with powder that the fingerprint team had used. The front room furniture consisted of a forties-style gate-legged table, and four high-backed chairs with leather seats. It reminded Josephine of the dining room furniture she had seen in her grandparents house when she was young. There was an old metal rail, with brass rings, fixed around the bay window with green brocade curtains hanging from it.

"God, I haven't seen one of those for years," Bill announced, as he reached up to examine it more closely, "Mind you they last a damn sight longer than the plastic rubbish you get nowadays. My rail in the flat is always falling down, this looks like it's been up for years!"

In the back room which overlooked the garden, there was an old leather pouffe and a brown tweed suite.

"Mum had one of these, I can remember there was no Dralon in those days," Josephine remarked as she looked around the room in deep thought. "You know Bill, according to Mr Kennedy, the Fieldings have lived here for about thirty years, so they must have moved here in the sixties. I'd say that they had bought new furniture when they bought the house, and maybe had stuff given to them by their parents. Some of these pieces are from the forties and fifties and others are from the sixties, which I have to admit I remember well."

"Well this bright orange carpet must have been fitted when they moved in, it's not in keeping with the rest of the place is it!" Bill noticed.

"Orange, black and white were popular colours in the sixties," Josephine said.

"You'd have thought she'd have done the place up a bit wouldn't you?" Bill added as he looked around.

"Maybe she didn't have the money, or the inclination. Remember she lived here all her life, she probably liked it the way it looked, and her mother only died six months ago, she probably wouldn't let her daughter change anything."

"I suppose you've got a point there," Bill agreed.

"Shall we go upstairs? Although I'm dreading

seeing that room again," Josephine said as she left the lounge.

As they entered the bedroom where two days earlier they had encountered the massacred, bloody body of Jane Fielding, it looked remarkably ordinary, apart from the chalk marks that outlined the body's former configuration on the bed, and the blood stains on the wall and carpet.

"Who the hell is he, and why did she let him in?" Bill asked despairingly.

"We don't know that much about Jane Fielding, let alone the murderer, as she seemed a loner."

"Well according to the reports that came in after the officers had made house to house enquiries, no-one else seems to know that much about her. No-one noticed anything unusual, no cars were parked that people didn't recognise, and no-one was acting suspicious."

"It sounds hopeless, surely someone must have noticed something," Josephine replied. "When we've finished here, I'll go next door and speak to Mrs Kennedy."

"I don't suppose she'll be able to add to what the husband told you," Bill commented.

"Possibly not, but she was the first one to find the body," she replied. She walked over to the large walnut wardrobe that stood in the corner of the room.

"Now let's see what we have in here. You'd be surprised at what a woman's clothes can reveal about her personality." She moved the hangers along the rail and examined the clothes carefully. "Mmm, that's quite revealing," she reflected.

"What is?" Bill sounded confused.

"All these clothes are a size ten to twelve, so I'm assuming that they all belong to Jane, as I think that her mother was quite a large woman. Now in this end of the wardrobe the clothes are dreary and old fashioned," she said as she removed a very old and dismal looking pale blue suit.

"They look alright to me," Bill remarked.

"They would!" Josephine uttered.

"I can't see what you're getting at."

"Look at this far end, there are three or four really smart outfits. Look at this short black skirt and this cream bodice, and look at this," she said as she held up a rather seductive-looking short red mandarin style dress that had a split up each side.

"I could see you in that, ma'am," he remarked.

"Be serious Bill!"

"Okay so there are two types of clothing, so what?"

"I'll tell you 'what'. We know that when her mother was alive, and Jane was nursing her, she didn't go out much. Do you agree?"

"I'm with you so far," Bill said.

"Her clothes were drab and old fashioned, but it didn't matter then. She didn't go out much. She didn't have a job, so she wasn't bothered about her appearance. Now suddenly she's a free agent, possibly with a little more money. Especially if her mother had left her something in her will, so she decides to splash out on some sexy stylish clothes. Why? Because she's going out more in the hope of finding someone. She's been alone for a long time, with no man in her life. I think that she was making a real effort to attract men. It was just unfortunate for Jane that she attracted the wrong one!"

* * *

"I'm glad that you're feeling better, Mrs Kennedy. You look well," Josephine observed, as she stirred her cup of tea.

"Yes I feel a lot better. I must admit, I thought that my time was up," Elsie Kennedy replied.

"As you probably know, my Sergeant Bill Hughes and myself spoke to your husband and he gave us quite a lot of helpful information, but there are still just a few things that I need you to go over with me, although I appreciate that it may be upsetting for you to recall."

"Please ask me anything you want to.

Obviously I'll never be able to forget that night. That scene will always be in my mind, but at least I am here to tell the tale. Poor Jane isn't. So I feel that if I can tell you anything that will put the monster who committed this crime behind bars at least I'll have done something," she announced.

"Thank you Mrs Kennedy. That's a very admirable and positive attitude from someone who has been through the ordeal that you have," Josephine declared. "Now I believe from what Mr Kennedy said that you had been concerned about Jane for a day or so."

"Yes. She'd often pop round, or I'd see her in the garden. Especially at the weekend."

"Could you tell me what happened when you entered the house?" Josephine asked.

"I'd got a spare key, as you know. We had known Jane and her family for years, and we were friends as well as neighbours. As I opened the door I shouted 'It's only Elsie, are you okay?' but I got no answer. After I'd looked downstairs I decided to go up to the bedroom."

"You didn't think that perhaps she may have just been out?" Josephine suggested.

"I didn't think, I suppose I thought she'd be in bed ill. As I reached the landing I saw that her bedroom door was open so I went in and that's when I saw..." Mrs Kennedy stopped talking. Her breathing became laboured and she reached to her throat.

"Are you in pain?" Josephine asked, looking quite concerned.

"I'll be okay. Just give me a minute," she uttered breathlessly. After a minute or so she seemed to recover and her breathing became steadier.

"When I saw her there and all that blood, I had a terrible pain in my chest, and the next thing I knew I'd passed out."

"I suppose that you knew that she was dead?" Josephine said.

"I must have done. If I hadn't have passed out I think I may have gone over to the bed where she lay. I used to do a bit of nursing in my youth so I don't really have a weak stomach but this..."

Josephine leaned forward and held her hand.

"I'll tell you something, shall I?" she began gently. "I've seen some sights in my profession, as you can quite probably imagine, but I just felt so sick that I had to go outside and get some air," Mrs Kennedy continued. "The next thing I remember was George trying to sit me up. He kept asking me if I was alright, but I could hardly speak, I just had to get out of that house. I couldn't wait there for George to phone for an ambulance and of course for the police."

"We don't seem to know that much about Jane, or why any one would want to murder her. We feel at the moment that it was just a maniac. I mean, had anyone been stalking her that you know of?"

Elsie Kennedy thought for a moment or so.

"No, I mean I'm sure that she wasn't worried or concerned at all."

"Can you tell us what she was like?"

"She was a very caring girl, which anyone can see by the way she looked after her ailing mother. She did have a job for a while, and I think she had the odd boyfriend from time to time, but while she was nursing her mother, she didn't have much of a life. I often offered to sit with Winnie so that Jane could have a night out, but she always refused."

"So what happened after her mother died?"

"Obviously she was very upset and depressed for a time, but then she started going out and seeing a bit of life. She started to take more pride in her appearance. She had her hair cut into a bob; Jane always had lovely thick brown hair but she had never really bothered with it in the past."

"I noticed that there were some quite new stylish dresses in her wardrobe," Josephine added.

"Did she have any friends that we could contact?" Bill asked.

"Not that I know of," Mrs Kennedy replied.

"Well thank you for your help. Please contact me if you remember anything else," Josephine said as she handed her card to Mrs Kennedy.

"I will, my dear," she replied as she looked at the card. "Oh, this says Detective Inspector, my word, and you're so young! I bet that your husband is very proud of you."

"I'm divorced, actually," Josephine said.

"Oh, I am sorry… still plenty more fish in the sea for a good looking girl like yourself."

Josephine felt elated as she drove home. *'Forty-four and she called me a girl. Maybe there's hope for me yet'* she thought. Then she realised that she hadn't contacted Andrew Blythe since their night out, and more to the point, he hadn't been in touch with her.

Chapter 7

JOSEPHINE WAS IN the forensic department waiting to speak to Gary Madison, who was in charge of the forensic team who had worked on the case. She had been in his office for about five minutes and had refused the offer of a drink from his assistant, when Madison came in from the lab.

"Sorry I kept you waiting Inspector. I've got the report here, but it's a bit of a nightmare, that's why it has taken so long," he said as he placed the file in front of her.

"Will you go over the main points with me in layman's terms?" she asked him.

"The trace was very difficult as the body was so bloody and had attracted a lot of debris. The fibres sent to us from Morrison, were a nightmare as they had to be cleaned before they could go under the microscope. The orange woollen fibres that we found match up with the carpet in the house."

"Is it possible she was killed or attacked somewhere else in the house?" Josephine asked.

"No, I think from the amount of blood in the bedroom that she was definitely murdered and butchered as she lay on the bed."

"Well that ties in with what Brian Morrison's report, that she was shackled to the head of the brass bedstead," Josephine said.

"We did find traces of blood on the stairs and also in the hallway carpet, but I think that this came from the assailant as it dripped from his clothing as he left."

"What about fingerprints?" she asked.

"Hardly any apart from hers. Either he cleaned up after himself or he wore gloves. The other fibres taken from thc hair and bloody areas of her neck and chest do not match with anything found in the bed or house. So I'd say that they came from her assailant, and there are quite a few. I'd say that we were lucky to find them."

"Can you tell what types of fibre they are?" Josephine asked.

"The substances vary. Some are nylon, wool, acrylic and also they're various colours. Some are red, others are blue, green and gold and so on. If these fibres did come from the assailant, it does seem strange that one person would have such a variety. Some could be from his clothing, some could be carpet fibres but none match up with the carpets in her house. Most people pick up fibres during the day at various times but they're usually brushed off. This is rather odd. Anyway it's all in the report," Madison said as he tapped the folder. Josephine picked up the file from the table in front of her and stood up.

"Good luck!" Gary Madison said as he smiled at Josephine.

"Thanks, I think I'll need it."

* * *

They were all assembled in the incident room, and the gruesome pictures of the mutilated body were pinned on the board. On the table lay copies of the report from the forensic lab, and also the report Brian Morrison had written. Josephine addressed the team.

"I gather you've all studied the reports. Now to go over the pathologist's findings. Time of death, anytime between eleven p.m. on Friday 30th August and six a.m. on Saturday 31st August, although it's difficult to pinpoint the exact time. There's no need for me to go through the horrific injuries the victim received, except to say that she had sex before she died. I stress the word sex as opposed to being raped by her assailant. Morrison could find no signs of forced entry which leads me to think that she knew the man and invited him into the house and possibly even asked him to stay the night. He is obviously sadistic and derived pleasure from her suffering. If you look at this picture…" she pointed to the victim's right hand and arm, which were a mass of small cuts. "These she received while she was trying to defend herself against the sharp blade. You can see by the marks on her wrists that both hands were originally shackled, we believe with handcuffs, due to the deep indentations on the wrists. It appears that one hand was released for a time possibly so that she could defend herself, although she must have known that she stood no chance of saving her life. Blood found under the nails was found to be the type A Positive. Jane's blood group was O Positive. It's almost certain that the blood found was that of her assailant," she turned to DS Bill Hughes, "Would you like to go through the Path Lab's report on the fibres found?"

"Oh… yes of course," Bill said, quite pleased that she had let him take charge of some of the proceedings. "Right, let's see…" He was a little unprepared, even though he had studied the reports in great detail. "Because the body was so bloody it had attracted several fibres. Some were found to be from the bed clothes and sheets and some orange fibres were from the carpet in the victim's house. The other fibres however, didn't match up with anything in the house, which means that they must have been carried in on the assailant's clothing. They were of various types. Some were wool, some acrylic or similar mixtures. The path lab found it unusual that anyone would be carrying so many different fibres on their person. I think that there may be a possibility that the murderer works with fibres, for example a carpet salesman or something similar. Now I know that this may be a long shot, but I'd like enquiries to be made at all carpet warehouses and retail stores. The man may live locally or he may come from the other side of the country. Barnes, can you and DC Peters organise the enquiries?"

"I'll get on it right away, sir," the DC replied.

Josephine walked over to the iced water machine, and poured herself a drink into a paper cup. She began to talk as she sipped it.

"Right, thank you Sergeant, I think that you may have a lead there. Well done. Now if we can go onto the victim's personality. In a nutshell, Jane Fielding was a bit of a loner, possibly due to the fact that she had to leave her job to look after her terminally ill mother, so consequently had little or no social life. However the situation appeared to have changed recently. She had been spending money on new clothes and on going out. I think that she may have met her assailant that Friday night or possibly previously. If that's the case they must have been seen at some pub or club in the area, so I want you four," she nodded at a group of PCs standing nearby, "To take a photo around the local venues and see if anyone saw Jane that Friday night. Let's just hope that he's local and that he hasn't left the area, otherwise our job is going to be difficult."

"I want the rest of you to carry photographs with you at all times," she pointed to a pile of photocopies which had been taken from an original photograph of Jane found in the house. "Unfortunately, since this photograph was taken she had had her hair cut and styled, so please remember to mention this to whoever you may show the photo to. Right then. Let's all get to work then, shall we?"

She picked up the files from her desk just as Inspector Cunningham walked towards her.

'Oh no, I suppose that I'll have to go through all this again with him.' she thought.

"Do you need me to go over the details of the case with you, Sir?" she asked.

"There's no need Inspector, I came in just as you began. I was standing at the back of the room. You seem to have everything under control."

Josephine was slightly taken aback. The Chief was normally so critical of her work and demanded up to the minute reports on a daily basis on any case she was working on.

"I know that you'll give it your best shot. As you know he has to be caught soon, otherwise the public will be panicking. Anyway, I came to tell you that the press are waiting in my office, I said that you would give them a statement."

'No wonder he's being particularly civil, he wants me to deal with them,' she thought, her anger welling up inside her.

"Are you coming too sir?" she asked him.

"Of course Inspector," he replied.

To say the press were in his office was an understatement! There were not just the local lads, but two reporters from the national papers, and a team from West Country Television. They descended on Josephine like a pack of wolves as she entered.

'He could have bloody warned me what to expect,' she thought.

"Right gentlemen… and ladies," the Chief said smiling at a young blonde woman from the local paper.

"I'm sure if you ask questions in an orderly manner befitting to your profession, Detective Inspector Blake here, will tell you what you want to know," the Chief stated.

"Is it true she was decapitated?" one reporter shouted.

"No," Josephine shouted back.

"And what about the rumour it's some religious cult, that has sacrificed her body?" another voice said.

"Rubbish," she replied again. The flashes from the cameras were hurting her eyes and she felt disorientated as they all continued bombarding her with questions. Her immediate reaction was to walk out of the room, but she doubted she'd get past them all and their equipment even if she tried. She felt exasperated and furious at their behaviour, but felt she must keep her composure.

"Be quiet all of you!" she bellowed. The room became silent. "I know you've all got a job to do, and you've got to take back some sort of a statement to your editors and producers. But I've got a murderer to catch, and you're not making my job any easier. I'll give you a statement if you comply with my wishes."

They all had their notepads and recorders at the ready and the television cameras started to film her. She hadn't got a written statement to read out, which was the normal procedure, but she began.

"Jane Fielding aged thirty two, lived at seventy three Hellaby Road, Barton, Torquay. She was murdered between the hours of eleven p.m. on Friday the thirtieth of August and six a.m. on Saturday the thirty first. She had been strangled, and stabbed several times, in what was a particularly brutal murder. She lived alone at the address, as she had lost both her parents. Her mother died about six months ago.

"Any idea who's responsible?" one reporter asked.

"It's far too soon to tell, we have a full report from the forensic pathologist, and we have derived certain information about the person we are looking for."

"Is the person local?" another reporter asked.

"It's impossible to say, we think the victim may have met him locally. Whether he's from this area, we don't know."

"Are women who live in this area safe?" someone shouted.

"As safe as they can be in today's society," Josephine replied.

"Can you give them any advice?"

"It's just common sense to be vigilant, not to walk home alone late at night, and not to answer the door to anyone you don't recognise, without identification," she felt annoyed by this last question and the feminist side of her came to the fore. "I'm sure most women are astute and intelligent enough to take care of themselves to ensure their safety, and don't need me to give them a list of do's and don'ts."

Some other questions were randomly asked by

the group in the room, but Josephine ignored them and said loudly and firmly "End of interview, I have work to do," and she pushed past one reporter, knocking his camera to the floor as she left.

"Right… thank you everyone, you're welcome to use our canteen for any refreshments you may require, before you leave," the Chief told them.

* * *

Josephine sat in her office drinking tea and smoking as Bill walked in.

"Congratulations, we heard you handled yourself very well with the media," he said.

"I could have handled it better if I'd have been prepared, and knew they were going to be there," she replied.

"That's the Chief, drops things on you like a bombshell," Bill remarked.

Josephine reflected for a moment or so, and then said "How did you know how it went? There was only the Chief and I in the office."

"He's been singing your praises around the station, he said you were co-operative, yet firm at the same time and you handled yourself well," Bill replied.

Just at that moment Andrew Blythe poked his head around the door.

"Hello stranger… or should I say 'Wonder Woman'?" he said.

"So you've heard as well," she replied smiling.

"Don't knock it Jo, it beats criticism, and you deserve it."

"There are some who wouldn't entirely agree with you," she replied.

Andrew sat in the chair opposite her, she thought he looked very attractive in his smart black suit and crisp white shirt, which contrasted sharply with his red and black patterned silk tie. Josephine suddenly wondered what she must look like, as she thought that the make-up she had applied earlier had probably all worn off. *'God if only I'd had known you were coming, at least I could have put a bit of lipstick on,'* she thought as she ran her fingers through her short blonde hair.

"Right, I'll get on now, I've got lots to do," Bill said and he left her in the office.

When they were alone, Josephine asked "Are you here on a professional matter or is it pleasure?"

"Well, you haven't been in touch about this latest murder case, and I didn't know whether you need a psychological assessment," he replied.

"Me or the killer?" Josephine joked in a sarcastic manner.

"Whichever you'd prefer," he replied, "I've read the file on the case."

"And what's your professional opinion?" she asked.

"I do need to study it in more detail, but I'd say he's obviously mentally disturbed to a certain degree, but you don't need me to tell you that. Anyway I'm sure you are tied up now, but when you've got the time, book an appointment with my secretary, and we'll go over the psychological aspects of the case. I'm due in court in an hour, I have to give evidence in the Marlborough case."

"So that's why you look so smart?" she observed.

"Don't I always?"

Josephine felt a little disappointed, that he had most probably called at the station in his professional capacity, and not solely to see her. *'God pull yourself together, you've only had one night out with the man, and you've got enough on your plate with this case without getting romantically involved!'* she suddenly thought to herself.

Just as he was about to leave, he said "I've found a quaint little haunt in Dartmoor, an eighteenth century inn; I'll pick you up tomorrow night, about eight shall we say?" He left before she had a chance to reply.

'What a bloody cheek, he's just taken it for granted I'd accept,' she thought.

Chapter 8

JOSEPHINE ARRIVED HOME at about seven o'clock that evening after calling into her local supermarket for some food. She had felt hungry all day, which was unusual, for normally when she was working on a gruelling case, she had little or no appetite. She had decided to buy some peppers, chicken pieces and noodles, and make herself a stir fry for supper. She'd also bought a good selection of cheeses and some garlic pâté from the delicatessen counter, plus two bottles of claret from the wine selection. This wasn't for consumption that evening, but for the following day, as she had decided to ask Andrew back for some supper after their evening out.

* * *

The sound of Puccini came from the compact

disc player, as she stood in the kitchen sipping wine. As she poured some Soya sauce into the wok, for some reason, just at that moment she felt quite content. The phone rang.

"Oh blast!" she shouted as she placed her glass on the table, and turned the heat down beneath the wok. *'I hope this won't spoil,'* she thought, as she turned the volume of the CD down with one hand, and picked up the phone with the other. Before she even had chance to say hello, a voice said.

"Hello, it's Tom."

"Oh," she said, surprised.

"How are you?" he asked.

"I'm fine, not that it's any of your business," she replied coldly.

"I saw you on the TV tonight, on the early evening news, you looked and sounded good."

"I haven't seen it, as I've only just got in."

"Have you heard from Jessica?" Tom asked.

"I think she's coming home for a few days at the end of the month, if she hasn't got much work on," she said to him.

"...Only Marion and I would like to take her out for a meal."

Josephine felt annoyed and hurt. She knew she wasn't being sensible and mature about the situation. Her daughter Jessica was twenty and at her last year of university, obviously she'd have to meet the new woman in her father's life sooner or later, but Josephine was jealous and couldn't bear the thought of it. It was almost as if Jessica was some small child, who could be enticed by sweets and toys.

"Well, you've got her telephone number at the flat. Ring her yourself," she snapped.

"Okay, I'll get in touch with her. By the way, do you remember the leaking roof in the conservatory?"

"I can hardly forget it, with the constant dripping noise every time it rains," Josephine replied.

"Well, I'm sending this friend of mine to fix it for you."

"I'm quite capable of getting it fixed myself," she announced angrily.

"Well it's been like it for months and you haven't done anything up to now, and he'll do it for free, as a favour, in return for some spare parts I got for his car."

"Alright, in that case I might as well have it done," she agreed, "When's he coming?"

"He'll ring you... Listen Jo, are you okay? I don't like to think of you alone in that house."

"Why not? It's never bothered you before, and I'm a big girl now, I can look after myself. Anyway I'm not alone, I've got a friend here, and I'm cooking him some Chinese food," she lied.

"Oh right, I suppose I'd better let you go then," he said disconcertedly.

Josephine put down the receiver and went back into the kitchen and took a large gulp of her wine.

'Bloody cheek, he's put me right off my meal now,' she thought, as she stirred the contents of her wok. Yet the second glass of wine gave her an appetite, and she ate two plates of Chinese chicken!

* * *

DC Sally James entered Josephine's office.

"We've had some information concerning Jane Fielding, from a Mrs Proctor who lives at number seventeen Hellaby Road."

"I thought we'd already spoken to all the neighbours," Josephine commented.

"That's right ma'am, we did in fact interview this lady several days ago, and although she knew Jane slightly, she hadn't seen anything unusual that could help us. It now seems however that her daughter, a Miss Sue Proctor, saw Jane leaving a nightclub in Torquay with a man, late Friday night. She says she didn't speak to her as she was on the other side of the road at the time."

"Why didn't she come forward sooner?" Josephine asked.

"Apparently she's been camping in Brittany

with friends for the last few days, she only heard of Jane's death when she returned two days ago."

"Well this is the best lead we've had up to now. Make an appointment for DS Hughes to speak to her. We need a description, the time she saw them, you know the procedure."

"Will do ma'am," Sally replied.

Just then Bill entered the office, carrying a large bunch of red roses.

"My word Bill, you're getting romantic, Joyce will be pleased," Josephine said.

"They're not for Joyce, they're for you, they were left at the front desk."

Josephine took the flowers from him and held the blooms to her nose.

"These smell lovely," she said excitedly. She opened the small note that was attached and it read,

Who's a clever girl then?

It was unsigned.

"Who are they from?" Sally asked.

"It doesn't say, but I've got a good idea who sent them," she replied. *'How romantic, a dozen red roses, Andrew must have seen me on the television last night and has sent them to congratulate me,'* she thought dreamily. She looked up and noticed Bill and Sally looking at her a little oddly.

"Right, no time to get mushy," she said, "Bill I need you to go and see a Sue Proctor, number seventeen Hellaby Road, we have what could possibly be the last sighting of Jane Fielding, before her death. Get as much information as you can about the man she was seen with, and see if she can remember enough about him to do a photofit. At least if we can get this man's photo distributed around the venues, there's a hope that someone might recognise him."

* * *

That evening Josephine left the station a little earlier, so she could indulge herself in a long hot bath, with some rather expensive aromatherapy bath oil that Jessica had bought her for her birthday.

As she lay there relaxing, she felt almost guilty that she was going for a night out. It hadn't anything to do with her ex-husband Tom, since he now had another partner, but more the fact when she was working on a murder case, it seemed to take over and there was little or no time left to socialise. It had always been this way for her, as she desperately needed to get justice for the families of the victims, and would work ceaselessly until they had caught the culprits. There was no doubt in her mind; Andrew Blythe was a very pleasant distraction, but she felt she should not really be seeing him.

An hour or so later, she had applied her make-up and blow dried her hair, and was in the lounge sipping a brandy, looking out to sea. It had been rather a sunny day, and the sky was streaked with red, as dusk approached. She had spent some time deciding what to wear, but finally settled on a taupe coloured trouser suit, and cream silk blouse. At eight o'clock the doorbell rang; as she stood up to answer it, she felt like a nervous teenager on her first date.

"Ready to go?" Andrew asked. Josephine looked over his shoulder and noticed he had left the car engine running.

"I'll just get my bag, and I'll be with you," she replied hurrying back into the house.

They sat drinking in the corner of a very cosy Inn, that had a roaring fire, even though it was a warm evening. It had low beams, with lanterns hanging from the ceiling.

"Are you hungry?" Andrew asked.

"No, I've already eaten."

"Only they make a great crab sandwich here, and I'm a bit peckish."

Josephine didn't mention the fact that she had got some food in for supper.

"Well go ahead and order one, don't mind me."

After he had returned from the food bar,

having given them his order, Josephine said "I haven't had chance to thank you for the flowers."

"What flowers?"

"Don't be a tease, the roses were gorgeous!"

"I'm not with you," he sounded confused.

"Someone sent me a dozen red roses with a note saying 'WHO'S A CLEVER GIRL THEN?' I just assumed it was you."

Andrew looked embarrassed.

"I wish it had been me, but it wasn't, I'm sorry Jo."

"There's no need to be sorry. Obviously someone, somewhere, cares about me," she said jokingly. "If I do have a secret admirer, I can't think who it can be. The card wasn't signed."

"I can't tell you who sent the flowers, but the 'someone who cares' is sitting next to you now," he said tenderly as he stroked her hand.

Josephine was flattered by his declaration, but also felt embarrassed and awkward. Andrew immediately sensed her uneasiness and changed the subject.

"How's the case coming along then?" he asked.

"We may have a lead, a neighbour's daughter did see her with a man, he could be her assailant. Jane was a bit of a loner, I'd say due to circumstances rather than choice, although since her mother died I think she was making an effort to go out and meet people. It's just tragic she met what appears to be a homicidal maniac."

"I agree, I've read Morrison's report, he's obviously very sadistic and brutal, and yet I think he also likes a challenge, that's why he untied her one hand, he must have derived great pleasure and satisfaction in watching her fight back."

"The fact that she invited him back, and had sex with him, shows she must have trusted him, or she was possibly more gullible and inexperienced than other women of her age," Josephine remarked.

"That may have been the case, but in my opinion, the killers I've come across appeared to be ordinary people on the surface who held down good jobs. They're even liked and respected by their neighbours. It's only when I've delved into their minds, I've discovered how deranged and mentally unstable they really were," he said to her.

Just then, the girl from behind the bar came over to their table with Andrew's order.

"This looks delicious," Andrew said as he bit into the crusty bread.

* * *

They arrived back at Josephine's house at around midnight. Josephine turned to Andrew and said, "I'd brought a few things in for supper, but I suppose you're not hungry now?"

"No," he replied, "But I wouldn't say no to a brandy"

In the lounge Josephine took two glasses and a bottle of brandy from the cabinet.

"I'd rather you have coffee if you're driving," she said.

"No, I fancy a brandy. I can always leave the car here and phone for a taxi to take me home," he replied. She poured two large drinks, and they went and sat on the chairs on the balcony. It was a clear night and the full moon shone over the sea.

"I can see why you can't leave this house," Andrew reflected, looking out to sea.

"I guess that's why you're a psychologist, because you can figure these things out," Josephine laughed teasingly.

"You know, you ought to laugh more often, it suits you."

"There hasn't always been much to laugh about," she reflected as she leaned back in the chair and closed her eyes, feeling the sea breeze on her face.

She felt his hand on her hair, and his face moved closer to hers. He touched her as if he had always wanted to, as his kisses smothered her face. Josephine responded; at that moment he was the only thing she cared about.

They left their clothes where they landed and made love until dawn, when they both drifted off to sleep.

When Josephine woke at eight a.m., Andrew had gone. She walked out on to the balcony and watched the sun spill over the hills onto the sea. She couldn't remember when she had felt so content and happy, and then, she cried.

* * *

DS Hughes was waiting in her office when she arrived.

"How did it go with the girl?" she asked.

"Not as well as I'd hoped. Sue Proctor was coming out of the Anchor Pub, by the harbour, with some friends. Apparently they were going to stay at someone's house, and then catch the boat the next morning and sail to France. As they were walking along she noticed Jane on the opposite side of the road with a man. She knew Jane slightly and would always speak when she saw her, although she'd only seen her once since her mother had died. Jane had asked her what pubs and clubs would be suitable for her age group, being in her thirties, she didn't want to go anywhere that was full of teenagers."

"Did she speak to her on that evening?" Josephine asked.

"No, unfortunately. She was going to cross over the road and say hello to Jane, but the crowd that she was with suggested that they went into the chip shop."

"What did she say about the man that she was with?" Josephine enquired.

"As it was dark and they were some distance away, she didn't really get a good look at him. All that she could tell me was that the man was dark-haired and that he was taller than Jane. She was about five foot four in height which could put him at anything between five six and six foot, I suppose. She thought he was wearing a light coloured jacket, but didn't see his face at all. She did see the back of his head, but that's not much to go on. I'm afraid that there's no chance of a photofit picture being put together."

"Did she notice anything about the way in which the man was behaving towards Jane. I mean, was he manhandling her in anyway?" Josephine asked.

"No, according to Sue Proctor's statement they were walking arm in arm, and she thinks that she heard Jane laughing, but she couldn't be certain."

"It doesn't seem very promising, does it?" Josephine said drearily.

"There's one thing that I've found out. Sue Proctor gave me a list of pubs and clubs that Jane frequented. It seems that there were only three. The

Black Cat nightclub, that plays a lot of sixties and seventies music and is frequented mainly by the over thirties. The Engine Pub that has a singles and divorced disco twice a week, and finally the Torbay Arms. You get a lot of professionals there. It's smart but the prices are extortionate, two pounds thirty for a pint, and three pounds for a glass of wine."

"How do you know?" Josephine asked Bill.

"I took Joyce there one night. Needless to say we only had one drink. There were loads of yuppies in there, not my sort of place at all."

"Well at least we've got something to go on, although some officers are visiting the pubs and clubs in the area with Jane's photograph. We can now concentrate on these three, and ask the staff if they remember seeing her there on Friday night; even if the barmen can't remember seeing her, most of the clubs and pubs have bouncers or doormen, they may remember her."

"I'll get onto that straight away," Bill said. "We've finished an extensive search of the area around Hellaby Road, including all of the gardens, but we've had no luck in finding the murder weapon."

"I didn't hold out much hope of us recovering the weapon, I think he's too clever to have just dropped it somewhere nearby. By the way, how's it going with the carpet shops and wholesalers?" she asked Bill.

"Nothing at the moment. It's like trying to find a needle in a haystack. Do you think that he's left the area?"

"No, I don't Bill. I've got a feeling that he's fairly local, don't ask me why. It's just a hunch."

"Well I just hope that you're right, as it might make things a little easier," Bill sighed.

* * *

When Josephine arrived home that evening there was a message on her answering machine from Jessica. She looked at her watch. It was six-thirty, *'she should be in by now,'* she thought as she dialled her daughter's number. After a few moments she got through.

"Hello Jessica, it's Mum here."

"Hi, how are things?"

"I'm fine, and you?"

"Working hard!" Jessica replied.

"I'm glad to hear it."

"One of my friends saw you on the television, but I was out."

"I didn't think that it would be shown in your area. Still, you didn't miss much," Josephine said.

"She said that you were really good. So you're dealing with a knife wielding maniac, be careful won't you Mum?" Josephine was touched by her daughter's concern.

"I will, don't worry. By the way, has your father been in touch?"

"No, why?"

"I think that he wants to introduce you to his new woman," Josephine said angrily.

"Oh… I see. Don't be bitter Mum. I'm sure that you'll meet someone eventually. You're not that old, and you can look okay when you make an effort."

"Well I'll say this Jessica, you can always bring me down to earth with a bump when I'm feeling happy."

"What do you mean?" Jessica asked, confused.

Josephine was tempted to tell her about Andrew but asked, "So when are you coming home?"

"End of next week."

"So is there a problem? Do you need any money?"

"No, I'm alright thanks. When are you going to use my email address? I gave it to you ages ago."

"You know I don't get on with computers Jessica."

"I've got to go now anyway, Tina's just cooked us all Spaghetti Bolognaise."

She hung up before Josephine even had chance to say goodbye.

Chapter 9

JOSEPHINE HAD BEEN at her desk for about fifteen minutes when Bill walked in.

"We've run through the computer all the shops, wholesalers, and carpet manufacturers in the area and we are getting them checked one by one, but as I said yesterday, nothing's come to light yet," he said to Josephine.

"I know it's a long shot, I mean we know that the assailant was carrying lots of fibres on his person, most of which were similar to the wool fibres found in carpets. I suppose there could be some other explanation for this, but it's all we have to go on at present," Josephine replied as she sipped her coffee from a paper cup. She pulled a face and shuddered. "This is rough stuff from that machine, but I couldn't be bothered to go to the canteen, and I desperately needed a dose of caffeine to wake me up."

Just at that moment DC Barnes came in looking rather pleased.

"I've got some information from the doorman at the Black Cat nightclub. I showed him Jane's picture, and he remembered her, in fact he said that she was a bit of a regular. It seems she used to go there about once a week, but always alone. He said that he always had a chat with her as he felt a bit sorry for her."

"Did he find it odd for a woman to go there alone?" Josephine asked him.

"I asked him that, he said that she seemed a bit nervous the first time that she'd gone there alone, but that she had made friends with some girls that she had met there, and used to have a dance with them, although she always left on her own. The best is yet to come ma'am. He says that he remembers her leaving on Friday night with a man," he paused for a moment to get out his notepad. He flicked over a couple of pages and started to read. "Not a very detailed description, but still. Approximately five-feet nine inches tall, medium build, he can't remember what he was wearing, thinks it may have been a suit; he's agreed to come into the station and do a photofit, but I don't think it will be very successful – he says that he can't remember any of the man's features."

"Still, he can look through the photos we have

on file, he might recognise one of them," Bill suggested.

"Did the doorman hear him speak, or notice how he acted towards Jane?" Josephine asked.

"No he didn't. The amount of people that they get in there on a Friday night must be near enough five hundred, it's a wonder he remembers any of them, unless he has to escort them from the premises. It seems that the only reason he noticed her that night was because Jane always left alone, and it was unusual to see her with a man."

"That description you gave us, Barnes, matches the one that Sue Proctor gave us of the man she saw Jane with by the harbour. I think that it's more than likely he was the man who went home with Jane and murdered her," Bill remarked.

"I suppose," Josephine began "But there's always the remote chance that she didn't invite him in and that someone else murdered her. Although as there were no signs of forced entry to the property it seems unlikely that this was the case."

She opened her desk drawer and took out a sheet of paper.

"Changing the subject for a moment, I've got Jessica's email address at university, although I doubt if I'll use it. I hate computers and I'm not technically minded at all," she admitted.

"I'll help you," Bill said as they walked towards

the computer. He started up the email program on the desktop of Josephine's Windows 98 machine. Before he could select the 'new message' button and enter Jessica's email address, a new message was displayed in Josephine's in-box.

"That's unusual. It must be some information from another station," she said. The message came up on her screen. The header said

clever girl

and the message was from

john666@hotmail.com

"This is a first for me. Not like you Bill. You get loads of messages from other stations, though I doubt that they're all about work, knowing you!"

Josephine felt the first stirrings of unease – the message was obviously not from another station. Bill lent over and selected the message header with the mouse.

The message appeared.

Who's a clever girl then?
Did you like the roses?
Roses the colour of blood
You're not as smart as you think

"God, Bill, look at this!" she shouted.

"My God, this is some sick bastard! But how did he get your email address?" Bill remarked.

Josephine, started to sweat, she felt shivery but

wasn't sure whether it was fear or the beginning of a cold, as she had had a sore throat for a couple of days.

"I wonder if it's one of the lads from another station playing silly buggers," Bill suggested, "And yet it's odd that the sender's email address isn't internal."

"I think it's him," she said shakily.

"Who?" Bill asked densely.

"Jane Fielding's murderer, Bill, who else could it be? My God, if he's the one who sent those roses…" she shuddered "And to think that they're at home on my table!"

"If you don't mind me saying ma'am, don't you think that's a bit melodramatic? I mean, the murderer," Bill replied in disbelief.

"I'll tell you what, I'll see if PC Collins is still on duty. He's a whizz kid with computers," Barnes intervened, and quickly left the room.

Some ten minutes or so later Barnes returned to the room with the PC in question.

"I hear you're good with computers. Is there anyway that we can trace who sent the last email message to me?"

"I can try and find out, ma'am." He sat down and inspected the message on Josephine's screen. After a few minutes the young PC turned to Josephine and Bill.

"I'm sorry ma'am but I can't trace the sender

from the address here."

"I thought you could always identify the sender from the address on their email account?" Bill queried.

"That used to be the case, sir, because to have an email account you had to have a computer and dial into your email provider with a modem. We actually located people by locating the phone they were using to dial in. Then people who wanted to stop their email being traced started using anonymous remailers – people who'd remove the identifying parts of the mail and substitute false ones."

"Why?"

"Many of them were sending material to Newsgroups that was illegal – either defamatory, obscene or violating copyright. But not all, or even most of them were used for that. One of the most public remailers was forced to reveal the addresses of people using his server by a law suit from the Scientologists. One of their most ardent opponents had used his services to distribute internal documents of theirs. And that remailer was in Finland!"

"So our man used a remailer?" asked Bill.

"No sir, worse. He used an internet based email company, Hotmail."

"Could you translate that into English for us, Constable," Josephine said wryly.

"To look things up on the world-wide web, you use a search engine – basically a piece of software that indexes everything on the internet. Many of them, such as Yahoo and Excite, offer email accounts that you can set up and administer through a web browser – the software that lets you view content on the web. The trouble is that they have no way of checking whether you're who you say you are, and many people use them as a safe way of sending dubious material over the net."

"But don't they still have to have a phone connection?"

"Yes, but not necessarily their own. They could be in a library that's offering internet access, a cyber café, a university – anywhere with an internet connection. And they can move around. This guy's used Hotmail, one of the first in this business. I've mailed them to ask about the account, but I don't hold out much hope. If the guy's clever enough to have anticipated this far, I doubt he's made any mistakes."

"Oh, I see," Josephine answered, both confused and disappointed.

"He obviously doesn't want you to know his address, ma'am," PC Collins added.

"Well, thanks for your help," Josephine told him.

"No problem, if I can be of any further help..."

"Yes, thank you Collins, I'll let you know."

The PC left the room, pleased that the DI had asked for his assistance.

"I don't suppose that he'd leave his address if he is the murderer. He's not that stupid," Bill remarked.

"I don't think that the word stupid should be used in any context when it concerns this man. I think that not only are we dealing with a sadistic and brutal murderer, but also a very clever and calculating individual. He's playing cat and mouse with us," she turned to Bill. "Get the Chief in here. He needs to know about this straight away. I won't leave the computer just in case he sends another message," Josephine said.

A few minutes later the Chief walked in with Bill.

"So you're saying that the message can't be traced. Are you sure?"

"We've had PC Collins in, Sir. He's got a degree in computer studies. If anyone could get the address, he could," DC Barnes told the Chief.

"I want this computer manned for the next few days. Bill says that this madman may have sent you flowers?" the Chief said to Josephine.

"Well according to the message, it looks that way," she replied.

"Then I think that you may be in danger."

"What, from a computer Sir? I doubt it."

"You're not taking this seriously enough, he may know where you live."

"I think that's unlikely, Chief."

"Well, he's got your email address, and he knows you're based at this station. He could easily follow you home."

Josephine's chest tightened as she began to feel afraid.

"I'll take extra care when I leave then, Sir," she agreed.

"We could put a PC outside your house," Chief Inspector Cunningham suggested.

"I'm sure that there is no need for that Sir," she replied. "Still, if he is the murderer, and we are not absolutely sure that he is, I hope that he contacts me again; through the computer that is, I don't fancy seeing him face to face."

"Well let's just be careful!" the Chief warned her and then left.

* * *

When Josephine arrived home, she was just about to put the kettle on to make tea, when there was a knock at the door. She opened the door, to find her neighbour Alfred standing there. He was a widower, who lived in the bungalow next door; he had lost his wife some two years previously. Due to her profession, and the long hours she worked, Josephine did not see him much, although they had always got on well, and he always kept a spare key to her house, in case she needed him to let anyone in.

"Hello Alfred, what a nice surprise, I haven't seen you in ages, the kettle's on. Will you join me for a cup of tea?"

"Well... if you're not too busy," he sounded hesitant.

"No, of course I'm not."

They went into the kitchen and she made a pot of tea.

"I'm sorry about you and Tom," he told her.

"Thanks Alfred, but these things happen."

"I know, when Lilian died I felt so lost and alone. There'll never be another woman for me," he reflected sadly, "Mind you, you're a lot younger, plenty of time to meet someone else."

She poured the tea, and opened a packet of biscuits, and placed a handful on a plate.

"I'm glad you decided to stay, and not sell up," he told her as he dunked a biscuit in his tea, "I wouldn't like to have lost a good neighbour, and apart from that you never know what sort of neighbours you'll get if you move house," Josephine smiled. "Oh, I nearly forgot," he continued, "There's been a man hanging about here today, carrying a red bag, it looked like a tool bag but I'm not certain."

Josephine's heart started to beat fast. "Did you speak to him Alfred?"

"No, I first saw him in your front garden, and then when I came out of my house, he disappeared, and I thought he had gone round the back to try your gate, but I know you always keep it bolted. Anyway I had a good look around but he was nowhere about."

"Did you see him get out of a car?" Josephine asked.

"No, I didn't... I'm sorry I can't be of more help," he said.

"If you see him again, will you phone me at work? I'll give you the station's number, and my mobile."

"Yes, of course I will, nothing's wrong I hope?"

She handed Alfred a card with the two telephone numbers on.

"No, but I just need to know if he calls again," Josephine lied.

They finished their tea and Alfred left. Josephine felt uneasy and anxious; and just at that moment the phone rang, and it startled her. It was Andrew Blythe.

"Hello..." she answered.

"Are you okay Jo? You sound strange!"

She told him about the message she had received via email, and her conversation with Alfred.

Andrew said seriously, "He's playing a cat and mouse game with you Josephine, and we're dealing with a highly dangerous individual, I'm coming around now."

"No, don't Andrew, I'll be fine."

"Why not?" he sounded hurt.

"I'm just really tired, I know it's early but I'm going to bed."

"Sure you don't want any company?" he asked.

"I'm sure, I'm whacked. Not that the other evening wasn't good for me, it was, but it's still early days after the divorce, I'm still confused and unsure of how I feel, and what with this killer, all I really need is a good night's sleep."

"Well, promise me you'll lock up properly, and take your mobile up to bed with you."

"Don't worry, I'll be fine, and the house is alarmed."

"I'll call you tomorrow then, and please take care."

Josephine put the receiver down. She checked the doors and windows vigilantly and then poured herself a large brandy, picked up her mobile phone, and went upstairs to bed.

She had been asleep for about an hour when the phone rang. She jumped up suddenly, and her head started to swim. She took some time before answering it.

"Hello, it's Tom."

"For Heaven's sake! What are you doing phoning me in the middle of the night?" she said angrily.

"What are you talking about? It's only nine o'clock," Tom replied.

"Oh is it?" Josephine looked at the figures on her digital alarm clock. *'I've only been asleep an hour, it seems like ages,'* she thought.

"I just thought I'd let you know, Gary called round today, about the conservatory, but there was no-one in."

Josephine was so relieved she started to laugh.

"Thank God for that!" she exclaimed.

"What's the matter, have you gone mad?"

She didn't bother to explain.

"Just tell him to get the key from Alfred next door, if he calls again," she told him and put the phone down. Josephine felt relieved and far more relaxed, as she drank the rest of her brandy. She fell into a deep sleep and did not wake until seven thirty the next morning.

Chapter 10

HER BODY WAS HEAVY and it was difficult to put her into the large cotton sack; the fact that she was so wet with blood made it even more of an encumbrance as her limbs were slippy and hard to manoeuvre. When he finally completed his task, he was exhausted. He poured himself a drink, still wearing the plastic gloves that were covered with blood. As he sat drinking his whisky, he watched the blood drip down the bottle he had just handled. Having rested for several minutes, his strength returned, which enabled him to drag the sack out of the kitchen and into the side garage. The most arduous part was lifting the sack into the boot of his car, as there was hardly any room between the car and the garage walls. When he had finally finished, he cleaned himself up, and backed the car out of the garage onto the drive. Shutting the garage door, he reversed off his drive, and began his journey.

When he reached his destination, the barber's shop, he drove down the side passageway to the rear of the shop, and dumped the sack. He was pleased with himself, *'He'd be very proud of my work tonight,'* he thought and he stopped at a pub on his way home to celebrate.

* * *

Martin Jones looked at the clock, it was ten-fifteen, and he was starting to get a little concerned about his wife Sheila, as she normally arrived home from her aerobics class at about eight-thirty.

'Perhaps she's gone for a drink with the girls,' he thought, trying to convince himself she was okay, and he was just being paranoid.

"Come on you, it's way past your bedtime," he said to his eight year old daughter.

"Oh Daddy, you said I could stay up 'til Mommy came home."

"I know that sweetheart, but I didn't think she'd be so late, and you've got school tomorrow."

After a few more moans and groans, the little girl agreed to go to bed.

"When Mommy gets in, if you're still awake, I'll send her up to kiss you goodnight," he told her.

"Alright Daddy. Goodnight and God bless."

After a few minutes, the little girl fell fast asleep. By midnight Martin Jones had contacted all his wife's friends by telephone, and when he had exhausted all other possibilities as to her whereabouts, he dialled 999.

Chapter 11

THE FOLLOWING DAY, Josephine was in the station by eight o'clock. She had slept well the night before, and felt fighting fit and resolute. She had coffee and toast in the staff canteen, and then went back to her office to do some paperwork, and make a few phone calls. She sat back in her chair, pleased that she had completed all the niggling little tasks that needed doing, and it was only nine thirty!

Josephine felt satisfied and content, until she suddenly looked over at her computer, and she became anxious and uneasy at the thought of logging into it to ask if there was any email for her. Although she knew it had to be done. She took a deep breath, as she sat in front of the keyboard and pressed the necessary keys; within seconds a message appeared on the screen.

You haven't worked it out yet josephine,
You were so good with the teddy bear murders.
You're not as smart as you think.
John

She was alarmed by this message. The Teddy Bear Murders was a case she had worked on two years previously, when a serial killer had left a teddy bear next to his murder victims. Obviously this man knew all about Josephine and her past cases.

Another message followed the first.

You've had one clue, now it's time for number two.
This one wasn't an orphan, but her child will be.
John

The message then ended.

'God, has he killed again?' she thought, as her heart pounded in her chest. Her fingers were so sweaty with fear they were slipping off the keys on her computer.

Josephine called an emergency meeting in the incident room, and the Chief was present with the investigation team. She went over the details of the message that had been sent to her computer.

"I don't know whether he's about to commit a second murder, or he already has, and we're too late," she said tensely.

"Despite the fact he may have committed only two murders, I think we are dealing with a serial killer, and he'll go on slaying his victims one by one until he's caught!" the Chief stated.

"It's all some sort of a game to him, he's playing cat and mouse with us, almost as if he wants to give us a fair chance to catch him," Bill added.

"I think we need more professional help. Let's get Andrew Blythe to study the profile of this case in more detail, and we also need to liaise with an expert on serial killers.

"I attended some lectures in London last year, given by Professor David Burke. He's one of the leading authorities in this field, and I think Andrew knows him," Josephine told them. "Now I know one of our PCs helped us the other day, but we do need to get hold of a computer expert, any suggestions?" she asked the team.

"There's a detective sergeant in our computer division in Exeter, who's first class. We've used him in the past to track down computer fraud cases. I'll contact him," the Chief told Josephine.

"Right, thank you sir."

Just at that moment the Sergeant who was on duty at the front desk entered the incident room.

"I'm sorry to disturb you Sir," he said to the Chief. "It may have no connection to the present case, but we have a missing person report."

"Give me the details," Josephine said abruptly.

The Sergeant read from the report sheet he was holding. "A Mr Martin Jones from nineteen Aran Drive, Paignton, has reported his wife Sheila Jones missing. It seems she didn't return home from her aerobics class last night, and according to her husband she is usually back between eight thirty and nine p.m. He's contacted her friends, who have told him she left them at about eight o'clock, and as far as they knew she was going straight home."

"She could have just had a night out with someone," Bill suggested.

"That's what I thought," the Sergeant replied. "But her husband was adamant his wife would never do such a thing. It seems she promised her young daughter she'd be back early to read her a bedtime story. From what he tells me, she's a very devoted wife and mother, and he thinks something's happened to her. I've contacted all the accident and emergency departments in the hospitals, but I've had no luck, so I don't think she has been involved in any sort of accident."

"Is he still here?" Josephine asked.

"No," the sergeant informed her. "He was anxious to get back to his daughter."

"Right Bill, I want you to go and see Mr Jones now. We'll need the route his wife usually took home from her aerobics class, and then arrange for a team of officers to search the area and make enquiries. There would be plenty of people about at that time of night, so someone must have seen her. Of course I realise we may be jumping the gun here, as she could arrive home, at any time, with a perfectly plausible explanation."

"I hope to God she does," the Sergeant remarked. "That poor man looked worried to death!"

After they had all left the incident room, Josephine telephoned Andrew, and for once managed to get through to him straight away. She told him of all the morning's events and asked about Professor David Burke. Andrew told her he'd contact him, and see if he could arrange a meeting as soon as possible.

Josephine's mind was full of ideas and notions that she had to sort out. She picked up all the messages that had been sent by the killer through her email, and decided to go home for an hour to study them.

Josephine sat on her balcony drinking tea; she read the messages again and again. The first one about the roses that said 'WHO'S A CLEVER

GIRL THEN?' That sentence she kept turning over and over in her mind, and she suddenly thought of a parrot saying 'WHO'S A PRETTY BOY THEN?'

She then scrutinised the second message: 'THIS ONE'S NOT AN ORPHAN, BUT HER CHILD WILL BE.' This led her to the conclusion that the person who he had already murdered or intended to murder, must have a child; therefore, he must have spoken to his victim. Maybe he knew them quite well, and they liked and trusted him. She shuddered with fear as she took another drink of her tea.

'ORPHAN... ORPHAN... ORPHAN... ANNIE,' she thought. She then looked at the date on her watch, as she recalled the date that the first murder occurred.

'Oh my God, that's it!' she thought. She was both frightened and excited, and she jumped up so suddenly she knocked her mug of tea off the table, and it smashed into pieces as it hit the slabbed floor. She went back into the lounge, and opened the door of her bookcase, searching frantically, until she found the book she wanted. She sat down and read it for about fifteen minutes.

"Yes, it must be the only explanation," she said out loud. She went over to her desk to get her address book, and quickly flicked through the pages until she found the telephone number she was looking for. Then she dialled Detective Inspector Mortimer at Scotland Yard HQ, as he was an expert on the killer that this man was imitating.

Chapter 12

TERRY ADLER CLIPPED away at his client's hair, it was his last appointment of the day.

"How's trade?" the man in the chair asked.

"Not bad. Of course, we've had one or two new unisex salons open in the High Street, but they don't seem to have taken away my trade. Some of my regulars wouldn't be seen dead in those places, as they still class them as ladies' hairdressers, and now I've got my new assistant," he said smiling at the pretty young girl who was sweeping up the hairs on the floor.

"So you're training her, are you?" the customer asked. Before Terry had chance to reply she said:

"He lets me shampoo the customers' hair, but won't let me near a pair of scissors, and I've been out of hairdressing college a year now!"

"I will in time Fiona, I've told you before. Anyway all the men love you washing their hair, they say you've got the 'gentle touch.'"

"Well if I don't get some of my own customers soon, I'm off," she told her boss.

Terry finished the man's hair and brushed his shoulders before removing the towel.

"There you are Sir, that will be four pounds fifty please." The man handed him the money and gave a pound tip to the girl.

"Make sure you don't let her go, otherwise you might lose my custom," he joked as he left the shop.

Terry Adler glanced at the clock on the wall. It was four thirty.

"I don't suppose we'll get anyone else in today. Empty the bins at the back and you can go home," he told Fiona.

"Okay, thanks Terry, but I meant what I said," she picked up two plastic bins and went outside into the yard at the rear of the shop.

As Terry was clearing out the basins he heard her scream; he took no notice to begin with, as he thought she'd seen a mouse. The sandwich bar next door often threw out stale food, and it attracted vermin; they'd already been warned by the Department of Health.

Her screaming didn't stop. *'It must be a rat this time,'* Terry thought, and he ran outside to see. His assistant was as white as a sheet, and just stood there pointing to a sack, that appeared to be soaked in blood. As Terry looked more closely, he could see what looked like an arm, protruding from the sack.

* * *

The police were there within minutes, and shortly afterwards Josephine and Bill arrived with two other officers. Brian Morrison arrived some thirty minutes or so later with the forensic team.

As Josephine peered into the sack, she could only see a mass of black hair through the mutilated and bloody limbs, but she had little doubt it was the body of Sheila Jones, despite the fact that it had not been formally identified.

She turned to Bill shaking with anger.

"I'll get this sick bastard, if it's the last thing I ever do!"

"Can you give us a rough time of death?" Bill asked Morrison. He looked at his watch, it was almost six o'clock.

"I'd say she had been dead about seventeen to twenty hours, that would be approximately between nine p.m. and twelve p.m. yesterday."

"If it's who I think it is, we'll have to contact Martin Jones to identify the body," Josephine said to Bill.

"When I spoke to him, he was out of his mind with worry. When he sees her I think he'll crack up," he replied.

"Let me try and clean her up first," Morrison began, "Although by the looks of her it's not going to be easy."

Despite the fact the crime scene was at the rear of the row of shops, a crowd had gathered. To the left of the barber's shop was the sandwich bar, and to the right a dress shop, and the staff from both shops seemed reluctant to leave, despite being asked several times by the police officers.

Luckily, the right of way at the rear of the shops needed to be wide enough for the trucks and vans to drive down as they delivered to the various shops, so there was enough room for the ambulance and police cars to get through. The area was cordoned off with tape to allow Morrison and the forensic team to work with some degree of privacy, although because they were outside, it did prove rather difficult.

Morrison told Josephine and Bill that a lot of the forensic evidence could have been blown or washed away, as it had rained earlier that day, which had wet the sack that Sheila Jones's body was in, making it even more bloody and sticky.

They left the forensic team to get on with their work and made their way back to the station. Josephine telephoned Martin Jones and asked if she could go and see him, but she did not mention that they had discovered a body, which she thought was that of his wife.

Some forty-five minutes later they arrived at his house. A pretty little girl, with a mass of black curls, opened the door to them.

"Hello," she smiled chirpily.

Her father walked up behind her, he looked pale and distraught; they followed him into the lounge, and the little girl tugged at Josephine's coat.

"Do you like my doll?" she asked as she lifted it up to show her. Josephine suddenly felt desperately sad, *'Oh you poor little thing'* she thought, and on impulse she picked the little girl up in her arms and hugged her tightly. It was both an unnecessary and unprofessional act on Josephine's part, but something she felt she needed to do.

"Why don't you go and fetch some of your other toys, only we need to speak to your Daddy alone," Josephine said gently.

"Okay," she said smiling, as she ran out of the room.

Martin Jones could see by Josephine's face, it was not good news and before she had chance to say anything, he slumped down into a chair.

"You've found her, haven't you?"

"We've discovered a body, that we think may be your wife, Sir, but we will need you to identify her," Bill intervened. He could see Josephine couldn't find the strength to tell him, as she was emotional.

"Er... okay... I'll have to make arrangements for Sophie..." he replied, in an obvious state of despair.

"I have a WPC in the car, if you would like her to stay with your daughter," Bill told him.

"No... she can stay with the lady next door, she has a son who Sophie plays with."

Just then Sophie came back into the room, her arms full of toys. Martin Jones suddenly picked up his daughter and hugged her tightly, causing her to drop all the toys on the carpet, and he cried pitifully.

* * *

He identified the body as that of his wife Sheila Jones.

"I'm so very sorry," Josephine said as they left the morgue.

"I can assure you, we'll do everything possible to catch your wife's killer," Bill tried to assure him.

"But you can't bring her back, and I can't live without her, I'm better off dead," he sobbed.

"Then what would Sophie do? She needs you more than ever," Josephine said as she touched his hand.

They drove him home in the police car, to a house that would never be the same again.

Chapter 13

AFTER ALL THE REPORTS had been received and the necessary people had been contacted, an emergency meeting with Chief Superintendent John Barlow was set up to deal with what the press had described as a 'Crisis'. They criticised the Torbay Police Department for the way the case had been handled. And they said the streets were no longer safe. This was an exaggeration, but quite typical of their tactics to sell newspapers.

Those present at the meeting with John Barlow were Josephine, Bill, and their Chief, Inspector Cunningham, Andrew Blythe, and his associate David Burke who was an expert in serial killers, and also Brian Morrison, and a computer specialist.

The Chief's room was bright and airy, and sunlight filled the windows; various plants were arranged around the room. After the usual introductions, they sat around a large, highly polished table, upon which they placed their various paperwork and files.

The Superintendent asked if anyone would like a coffee, but nobody did. They all seemed eager to get on with business. Josephine looked over at John Barlow; he was still an attractive man, even though he was nearly sixty. He had a few grey streaks in his black hair, and a remarkable physique for his age.

The Superintendent began,

"I think there is little if no doubt, that these crimes were committed by the same person, and I think it's safe to assume that he's also responsible for sending messages to Detective Inspector Blake's police computer by email."

They all nodded in agreement.

"Needless to say, the man is extremely dangerous and his crimes are horrific. I'm no psychologist, and I leave that area to the experts," he said looking in the direction of Andrew Blythe and David Burke. "But it's obvious to me he gets tremendous satisfaction from butchering his victims." He turned to Josephine, "If you could briefly give us the details to date, before we have the forensic report on the latest victim."

"Yes, certainly sir," Josephine stood up to address them all.

"The report you all have in front of you, covers the finer aspects and technicalities of the case, but the brief details are as follows. Victim number one, Jane Fielding, lived alone in Hellaby Road, Torquay. She was found stabbed and strangled, by her neighbour on Sunday thirty first of August. Forensic reports show she was shackled to the brass bedstead with handcuffs. We think she met her assailant at the Black Cat nightclub, and invited him back to her house, as there were no signs of a break-in. We do have two sightings of the man we believe to be her killer. One by a neighbour, and the other by the doorman of the club in question. You all have a photofit of the man, but as you can see there are no particular distinctions, he looks stereotypical and could be almost anyone – neither person managed to get a good look at his face. Nevertheless the photofit is being circulated. A considerable amount of fibres, possibly from carpets, were found on the victim. We did think that it was possible that the killer may have worked in the carpet trade, as it seems unusual for one person to be carrying so many different fibres. Unfortunately investigations carried out so far in carpet shops and warehouses in the area have proved fruitless.

"Now we come to the second victim, Sheila Jones, who again was strangled and butchered in a similar way, obviously the work of the same man. We believe the woman was accosted on her way home from an aerobics class. She was murdered and mutilated in a different place from where her body was found. We think her murderer put her into the sack and then transported her, possibly in a car, to the rear of the barber's shop on the High Street, Torquay, and dumped the body there," Josephine had given her report in a cool and professional manner, but then became emotional.

"She was married and had an eight year old daughter. The family are devastated. We must catch him before he kills again!" She started to tremble and her voice faltered.

"Thank you DI Blake," the Chief Superintendent intervened. "Now I think we all need some coffee before we continue."

They were served coffee and biscuits, and David Burke asked if anyone would mind if he smoked. No one objected, so he lit a cigarette and offered Josephine one, which she accepted.

After several minutes had passed, the Chief asked Brian Morrison if he'd give them his report on his findings after examining the bodies.

"As DI Blake informed you, tests carried out on Sheila Jones's body showed time of death at approximately between nine and twelve p.m. on September the eighth. After she was murdered, she was put into a sack; it must have been a difficult task, as she was quite a big woman, and due to her injuries she had lost a large amount of blood, which would have made the body wet and awkward to manoeuvre. The only way he could have transported her to where the body was found was by car, as it would have been virtually impossible to have carried her for any distance, unless there were two or more people involved. As with the first victim, she was strangled before the body was cut about. The abdomen was laid open and the uterus was partly removed, and she had stab wounds over her entire body. If she hadn't been dead before he carried out these mutilations, she'd have been in such excruciating pain, that her screams would have been heard from some distance away. There were no signs of sexual interference on Sheila Jones' body, and although we did find semen in Jane Fielding's body, which shows she had sex shortly before she died, I think she consented to it, as there were no signs of injury which would indicate rape. The fibres found on Sheila Jones' body were very similar to those found on Jane Fielding's, although we didn't get an exact match on any one fibre. The sack that contained the body had lain there overnight, and due to the wet weather, some of the evidence and fibres were destroyed. But because she was in the sack some of the fibres were protected, so still detectable."

"Would you say the murderer had expert medical knowledge. I mean could we be looking for a doctor or surgeon perhaps?" John Barlow asked.

"I don't consider the surgery performed on the bodies to be skilled. The murderer may have had a little knowledge of the human anatomy and just hacked at the body with great force, causing some organs to be partially removed."

"Can we determine the sort of cutting instrument used?"

"A sharp cutting instrument with a single edge, which unfortunately could be just about any type of knife," Brian Morrison replied, as he closed his file. "That concludes my report, Sir."

Detective Sergeant Bill Hughes raised his hand to attract the Chief Superintendent's attention.

"Yes, Sergeant?" he said when he noticed him.

"May I just add Sir, that despite the fact we carried out an extensive search in the surrounding areas of both crimes, no weapon was discovered. DI Blake and myself think both crimes were committed in the privacy of a house. In the case of Jane Fielding, in her bedroom. And we think Sheila Jones may have been abducted and taken to the assailant's home, or some other private building where he wouldn't be disturbed, so he could murder and mutilate his victim, before transferring her to where the body was discovered."

John Barlow listened to Bill and then said, "Now if we can move on to the fact that the killer has been contacting DI Blake by email at the station. You all have a copy of the messages sent. What's your psychological assessment of the killer Doctor Blythe?"

"I believe our killer has developed some sort of attachment to Josephine," he began; he unlike the others had referred to her by her Christian name. "He happened to mention a past case she was working on, the Teddy Bear serial killer. DI Blake and her team worked on that case in nineteen ninety-six, so he's either just remembered reading about it in the newspaper at the time, or more likely he's been following her career. Also the fact he has sent her roses, and he's giving her clues to his crimes, points to the fact he's playing an elaborate game with her, but possibly sub-consciously he almost wants to be caught. I have also come to the conclusion that her life may be in danger!"

"Do you have any views on this?" John Barlow asked Chief Inspector Cunningham.

"I agree with Doctor Blythe here, and I have recommended DI Blake have protection, but she has refused it."

"Is this correct?" he asked Josephine.

"Yes Sir, I have in the past been reluctant to

have protection. I am a policewoman, and I'm supposed to be able to look after myself.

John Barlow said in a serious voice, just like a father figure, "Now listen DI Blake, I've had a few bravery awards during my forty years in the police force, and quite frankly, if I came across this man I'd be frightened. We're dealing with a maniac, but you don't need me to tell you that. If you don't agree to police protection, I will have no alternative but to take you off this case." He finished talking and waited for her reply.

"Then I will comply with your wishes, Sir," she agreed.

"Right, that's settled," John Barlow stated.

He was just about to pass over to the computer expert when Josephine said, "I have some additional information that I'd like to tell those present, before we continue."

"If you feel it is relevant, then please go ahead," The Chief Super agreed.

What she was about to tell them, came as a complete bombshell, out of the blue. She had been doing some research with an associate in London, but had not told the team about her work. She knew this was unethical, but felt she had no option until she was sure of her findings.

"I'd like to ask someone else to sit in on the meeting, if I may Sir?" she asked John Barlow.

"Who would that be?" he asked.

"It's a Doctor Roger Graham."

"What is Doctor Graham's particular field in police work?" he asked.

"I feel I cannot disclose that information Sir, until I have gone over certain facts with everyone present."

John Barlow was somewhat displeased with her reply, but nevertheless said. "Very well Inspector, but let's please get a move on."

Josephine gave everyone seated around the table a folder.

"I'd ask you not to open the folders and read the information enclosed until I have finished," she requested.

Bill was concerned and a little annoyed as he thought Josephine was pushing her luck a bit too far with the Chief Super, *'I hope she gets to the point, and pretty damn quick, before the Chief loses his temper,'* he thought.

Josephine walked to the door, and after a moment or so a man entered. He was quite small in stature, with mousy coloured hair and was in his fifties. Not at all the person they had expected!

"I'd like to introduce you to Doctor Roger Graham," Josephine announced. He quickly glanced and nodded at those present and then he sat down.

Josephine began, "I shall try and get to the relevant point as quickly as possible. Now as you know, the first contact from the killer, so to speak, was when he sent the roses to the station with a card which read: 'WHO'S A CLEVER GIRL THEN?' I must admit I did think they were from a friend," she said glancing at Andrew for a second, "Congratulating me on my TV appearance the night before. It was only when the same message appeared on my email, I realised they were from the killer. I will just hasten to add, the card attached to the flowers is now being examined by a handwriting expert. The second message, sent before Sheila Jones's body was discovered read: 'THIS ONE'S NOT AN ORPHAN, BUT HER CHILD WILL BE,' which led me to believe he knew the woman he had killed, or was about to kill, had a child, so he may have been someone she knew."

"I can't see where this is leading Inspector, please get to the point," the Chief urged her.

"Right, Sir. I don't need to repeat that these were particularly bloody and sadistic murders, where the victims were butchered. The first message – 'WHO'S A CLEVER GIRL THEN?' – sounds similar to the conventional idea of what a parrot might say – 'WHO'S A PRETTY BOY THEN?'.

The people seated around the table looked at each other and then at Josephine. They all seemed to be harbouring a suspicion that she'd gone mad. Nevertheless she continued.

"Right, let's take a chance that this is a deliberate clue by the killer. Polly is a common name for a parrot. Now, forensic evidence shows that the death occurred on Saturday the thirty-first of August. Moving on to the second message, 'THIS ONE'S NOT AN ORPHAN...' there's a saying, 'Orphan Annie,' that I'm sure you're all familiar with." One or two people nodded in agreement.

"Despite the fact the body was not discovered until the evening of the ninth of September, tests show she died the day before, on the eighth. Mary Ann Nicholls was savagely murdered on 31st August 1888, and was known to everyone at the time as 'Polly Nicholls'. Annie Chapman was found murdered and mutilated on 8th September 1888 and her body was found behind a barber's shop at number 29 Hanbury Street, Whitechapel, London. Sheila Jones was discovered at the back of a barber's shop in Torquay. After consulting with Doctor Graham, who is an expert in this field, I think we have a copycat Jack The Ripper killer!"

There were gasps of shock at this pronouncement.

"I'd like to introduce Doctor Roger Graham, who has for many years studied the notorious Jack The Ripper, and has written many books on the subject."

Doctor Graham stood up, although he was small in stature, his voice was deep and commanding.

"After having studied all the information, times, dates and messages sent in detail, given to me by Detective Inspector Blake, I agree with her interpretation, and in my opinion, it is the most obvious conclusion. If you now open the folders that were given to you by the Inspector, you will see enclosed a brief history of Jack The Ripper probably the most notorious and infamous killer of all time! If you turn to the first page, you'll see a list of his victims. There were another two similar murders committed before these dates, although they were never proven to be the work of Jack The Ripper."

The first page read:-

THE VICTIMS

- POLLY NICHOLLS: 31st AUGUST 1888, BUCK'S ROW, WHITCHAPEL.
- ANNIE CHAPMAN: 8th SEPTEMBER 1888, HANBURY ST, SPITALFIELDS.
- ELIZABETH STRIDE: 30th SEPTEMBER 1888, BERNER ST, WHITECHAPEL.

- CATHERINE EDDOWES: 30th SEPTEMBER 1888, MITRE SQUARE, ALDGATE.
- MARY KELLY: 9th NOVEMBER 1888, MILLER'S COURT, DORSET ST, SPITALFIELDS.

"As DI Blake has pointed out, the first two dates and names match up," he told his astonished audience.

"My God, do you think he'll go down the list until he's killed them all?" Chief Inspector Cunningham uttered.

"I think he will, unless we can catch him in time," Graham replied.

"The twisted and mysterious killer known as Jack The Ripper has become more of an enigma as time passes," he continued. We know for a fact that he butchered five women – some say more. Most of these were prostitutes. The population as a whole were panic stricken, not just those living in Whitechapel. The police at the time were powerless. There have been literally hundreds of books written about him over the years, and even a book purporting to be his diary has been published – a hoax. There were certain suspects, but no-one has ever discovered his identity. Many notions and theories have been put forward, but none seem to have bought us closer to the truth.

Despite the fact the Ripper has been dead for many years now, his unsolved crimes exert a grim fascination on the imagination of many – there are even magazines published dealing with him and his crimes."

He paused for a drink of water from a nearby glass, before continuing.

"I think your killer is completely absorbed and obsessed by him. In his mind Jack is his hero, and he feels that by copying his crimes he is honouring his memory. Perhaps he isn't skilled enough to mutilate the bodies as exactly as his idol, perhaps his victims aren't prostitutes, but he's trying to mimic him as closely as he can."

"Jack The Ripper wasn't the first serial killer, and there have been periods when his crimes were overshadowed by those even more brutal," the Chief interjected. "The Texas Ripper alone killed nine women between 1884 and 1885. Even in the present day there have been more horrific crimes – Nielsen, the Yorkshire Ripper, Ian Brady and Myra Hindley – so why is he so special?"

"I think it's because he struck at a time when London's police were under a great deal of criticism. People had little or no faith in them. He terrorised London, which was the premiere capital city of the world at the time, and he reduced it to panic and terror. You must remember that, for the time, he attracted a huge amount of press coverage – he may not have been the world's first serial killer, but he was the mass media's first serial killer. By comparison the Texas Ripper was hardly known. The unpopularity of the Metropolitan Police at the time cannot be overestimated. Sir Charles Warren, who headed the force at the time, was the most hated man in London, and the newspapers damned his career. Inspector Abberline, well liked, an experienced East End policeman who had served in Whitechapel for fourteen years, hadn't the faintest idea who the Ripper might be."

"Isn't it significant," Andrew Blythe said, "That the murderer is setting DI Blake a challenge to catch him? Since so many detectives at the time of the Ripper murders failed to catch him, despite being taunted by him, and despite him committing the murders in a geographically small area. Isn't that why he's sending her these clues by email – it's a further attempt to replicate the conditions of the original killings?"

"I agree," Doctor Graham replied.

He picked up a file the table.

"In your files you'll find a complete dossier on the original killings. The police photos of the victims, the sites where they were found and a list of contemporary suspect, plus other information I consider relevant. Josephine has made certain every one of you has copies of this information. I suggest you study it for any clue, however small, that might aid you in your current investigation."

"Doctor Graham does have to return to London, but will be available for consultation at any time, night or day," said Josephine.

The Chief Superintendent stood up.

"Well, despite the fact that you surprised us all, and kept us on tenterhooks, it was well worth the wait." The Chief smiled at Josephine. "I'd also like to thank you for the time you've taken in making up these dossiers for us, Doctor Graham. Now we seem to have established that our murderer is a Jack The Ripper copycat, and a serial killer. What are your views on what you've just heard, Professor?" He directed the question to David Burke, a forensic psychologist with expertise in the field of serial killers.

"There are hundreds of thousands of ordinary people who are both obsessed and fascinated with Jack The Ripper – this is obvious from the vast quantity of books in print about him. Most of these people are interested in the puzzle element – in many ways it's one of the last great unsolved mysteries of our time. What does it take to turn that interest into a desire to kill? There have been other killers who have exhibited similar characteristics to him in the past – but never one so obsessed that they would stick to the exact dates of the original killings. My conclusion is that we can expect another killing on the thirtieth of September."

'It's the fifteenth today!' Josephine thought to herself. '*We don't have much time!'* She looked at the pad in front of her and realised with a sudden lurch in the pit of her stomach that the original Ripper had killed *two* on that date. She looked up as David Burke continued.

"The serial killer gets tremendous satisfaction from taking a life – the screams of his victims make him feel intensely alive. He plans his murders in minute detail, and also plans the clues he sends to DI Blake by email. Suffering and death almost certainly give him sexual pleasure. Serial killers aren't exclusively a twentieth century phenomenon, as Jack The Ripper proves. In my experience they often seem quite nice, ordinary people on the surface – they could be your friend, neighbour, brother. How often have we heard, after a particularly hideous crime has come to like 'He seemed such a nice man', 'They seemed so ordinary'?"

"The best probability is that this man is white, single and between the ages of twenty-five and fifty. He's probably quite charming – he may even seem shy or sensitive. But he has an ego as big as a planet. I think he wants to be caught, although he may not even realise that himself – but that's why he's sending DI Blake clues. He wants publicity, his picture in the paper, and recognition for his crimes. He probably wants to be more famous than Jack The Ripper, who, in his eyes is his hero, his God. If he's never caught, he won't be."

"What I can't understand is why he's committing his crimes in Devon? I'd have thought he'd have gone to Whitechapel in London, or whatever the area's called these days," Josephine said.

"If he's a local man, which there's a good chance of, it's better for him to commit his crimes in an area he's familiar with. He may even have used his own home to mutilate Sheila Jones. Apart from which, if he's been following your career for the last few years, he knows what cases you've worked on, and how you've tracked the killers. He's probably only got his information from newspapers; we know he wants fame and you've had more press coverage than most round here, due to the high profile of the cases you've been involved in. Now the challenge for him is to pit his wits against you."

Barlow stood up to close the meeting.

"I'd like to thank you all for your hard work and commitment. I'm sure you'll all agree we should keep much of this between the people in this room. If the press get hold of this theory it could cause unnecessary panic. I can see the headlines now: JACK THE RIPPER TERRORIZES TORBAY!"

"I can see your point sir, but I think they may be on to it already. They don't know about the emails I've received from the killer, but they've got the dates and know the method of murder. As we've discussed, fans of Jack The Ripper are everywhere – they've even got a term for it – Ripperologists. It won't be long before someone, either a reporter or just someone watching the news will put two and two together. Doctor Graham tells me there are people who watch for crimes on these dates, because they believe both the murders and the dates have mystical significance. It wouldn't take much for one of them to decidc to earn a bit on the side from the national press."

"Point taken Blake, point taken."

* * *

The next morning the first newspaper to land on Josephine's desk had the headline:

JACK'S BACK!
RIPPER STALKS STREETS OF DEVON

* * *

When Josephine arrived back at the station with Bill, she felt physically and emotionally drained. She suspected Bill must be feeling the same, as he hardly spoke on the way back in the car. It was almost six o'clock in the evening, and they had hardly eaten all day.

"Shall we get a curry or a Chinese take away, my treat?" Josephine suggested.

"I'm not hungry," Bill replied.

"That's unlike you, you're normally ravenous. Well I don't know about you, but I could certainly do with a drink. Shall we go to the Plume and Feathers?" The pub in question was about five hundred yards from the station, and was frequented by the police force. Bill didn't answer her question.

"Okay Bill spit it out, what's wrong?"

"Nothing," he replied.

"I've known you long enough to know that nothing means everything. Come on out with it."

"I'm amazed I need to tell you. You go behind my back and consult that chap about the Ripper," he began.

"If you're referring to Doctor Graham, he's a expert, as well you know," Josephine replied.

"That's not the point, you could have discussed the messages with me and we could have sorted it out together."

"I didn't mean to exclude you from my investigations Bill; one day I just kept mulling them over again and again, and something just clicked. There were similarities to Jack The Ripper, I remember I'd bought a book some time ago about him, but never got around to reading it, and when I went through it the names and dates just seemed to fit. I wasn't sure at the time that my idea wasn't a bit too far fetched, and that my imagination was getting the better of me. I was tempted to go through my ideas with you, but instead I rang DI Mortimer at Scotland Yard, he's been fascinated with the Ripper for some years, and he put me in contact with Roger Graham."

"Okay, I can appreciate you wanted to be certain of your hunch before you told me, but you could at least have said something before we went into the meeting. I mean it looked like I'd been liaising with you, and I didn't know a damn thing about it!" Bill said.

"I suppose it was a bit dramatic, me dropping it on everyone like that, I guess I just wanted to surprise you all," Josephine admitted.

"Well, you certainly did that," Bill replied.

"I haven't got a reasonable explanation, as to why I didn't tell you Bill, I've been a bit confused lately, both in my private and professional life, but I can assure you it wasn't because I didn't trust you. In fact I do confide in you more than most people Bill, and I'd like to think you were my friend." Bill was silent for a few moments and then said,

"Alright, now you've explained the situation, I sort of see your point, I don't suppose you meant to exclude me, and you've been quite good to me since I split up with Mary," Josephine smiled to herself, she had known Bill long enough to realise this was quite an emotional offering of the olive branch; from a man who rarely showed emotion.

"So am I forgiven?" she asked him.

"Mmm... I suppose," he grunted.

"Well, can I buy you a meal then?"

"Okay, if you insist," Bill replied.

They sat in the Indian restaurant looking at the menu, as the waiter placed two glasses of lager on the table, and asked if they were ready to order.

"I'll leave it to you," Josephine said.

"Right we'll have two medium Baltis with naans, pilau rice, oh... and I'll have a shish kebab and a few poppadoms to start, with dips." After the waiter had taken the order Josephine said,

"I thought you weren't hungry."

"Well if you're paying, I might as well have what I fancy," Bill said grinning.

Chapter 14

THE FOLLOWING MORNING Josephine briefed the team on everything that had been discussed at the Chief Superintendent's meeting, and she gave each of them a file with all the relevant information that Doctor Graham had compiled. She told them of her conclusion that they were dealing with a copycat killer. They all seemed quite alarmed, and yet at the same time excited.

"Concerning Sheila Jones's murder, I want the two friends that she went to the aerobics class with interviewed and statements taken. If it's possible she knew her assailant, they may have seen her talking to him. See if they can remember Sheila mentioning anything that might be relevant," Josephine turned to Bill.

"What's the name of the club?"

"It's the Harbour Fitness Club."

"Right. Barnes – I want you and DC James to

go over there right away, and get a list of all the members. I doubt that the killer was a club member, but someone might have seen something."

She then turned back to Bill.

"Who's our family liaisons officer at the moment?"

"It's DS Anthony Knight."

"Right, arrange for him to visit Martin Jones, I want to know if he can recall his wife mentioning anything. He'll need to be treated with kid gloves, as he's been through a terrible ordeal and so has the child. The liaisons officer will be more experienced at dealing with him than we would."

"The husband's asking when her body can be released for the funeral."

"Not yet I'm afraid, Morrison needs to make sure he hasn't missed anything that could be vital to the case. By the way, when's Jane Fielding's funeral?"

"Next Wednesday, although I doubt there will be many there," Bill replied.

"We really ought to attend, check if we've got anything on that day," she said.

"Will do ma'am, oh by the way, since the team are no longer needed for house to house enquiries in the Hellaby Road area, I've appointed them to cover the shops in the High Street where Sheila Jones's body was found."

"Thanks, I'm glad that's in hand, but to be honest since the body was probably dumped in the early hours of the morning at the rear of the shop, I doubt if there would be anyone around at that time. Still I suppose there's always a possibility of someone seeing something. We'll have to put any additional information we get into the HOLMES computer, as the size of the enquiry is now bigger than we originally anticipated. He could be making plans now for victim number three on the thirtieth of September, and the most frightening part is, if he's following the Ripper's crimes to a tee, he'll kill two on that day, unless we catch him in time. Check with the other police forces, to see if they've had any similar crimes committed, although I think he's just sticking to this area."

She walked over to the iced water machine and poured herself some in a paper cup.

"I think we should hold another press conference."

"They're like a pack of wolves waiting to pounce, at the moment, and they're not doing the force much good with their constant criticism," DC Barnes stated.

"I don't need to tell you, I agree with everything you've said, but I feel we must work with the media as I want to appeal for witnesses, both in the paper and on TV. Someone, somewhere, must have noticed Jane Fielding leaving the nightclub, and Sheila Jones walking home from the Harbour Fitness Club," Josephine remarked.

"In one statement," Bill began, "Her friend Jean Lock said she left the girls at about eight thirty, turning down their invitation to go for a drink, as she didn't want to miss her bus. The next bus that went to her home was a number seventy two, that leaves the Strand at eight forty-five, it's about a ten minute walk from the club to the bus stop. I think that she was abducted there, so surely someone must have seen her, as it was quite early."

"If we can get the family liaisons officer to get a fairly recent photo from her husband, we can show it in the press and possibly on the TV in the hope it may jog someone's memory, and also the photofit picture that was made up from the description we had from the doorman at the Black Cat nightclub, although it's not very reliable. We need both the media's and the public's help if we are to catch this man in time," Josephine announced.

When the briefing was over, Josephine went back to her office and kicked off her shoes. Her head and neck ached. Opening the desk drawer, she took out a bottle of paracetamol, and swallowed two tablets, swilling them down with a bottle of spring water she kept by her desk. She closed her eyes and massaged her temples and was just starting to relax as the pain eased, when the phone rang. It was Andrew Blythe.

"Hi, how are you?" he asked.

"I've had better days; come to think of it, I've had better years."

"My word, you sound depressed," he commented.

"I've been checking my email every hour in the hope he may send a message, but nothing has come through as yet," she told him.

"I'm worried about you, Jo."

"There's no need to be, he can't harm me through a computer," she replied.

"So you think he'll just be content with that? Because I don't. Sooner or later he'll want to confront you in person."

She felt cold inside and vulnerable like a small child, but said "Well if he does, at least we may catch him then."

"At what expense? Your life!"

"Stop it Andrew, you're frightening me."

"Good, that's my intention because until you realise you're in danger, you won't take the necessary precautions."

She knew he was talking sense.

"Okay, I'll get something organised with the Chief, if you insist," she snapped.

"For God's sake Jo, it's only that I care about

you," he said as he slammed down the receiver.

'What the hell's wrong with me?' she thought *'Tom's not bothered, now he's got a new woman in his life, and Andrew's the only one who cares about me, and I'm so abrupt and nasty. I must ring him back.'*

Just as she was about to dial his number, a PC came into the office.

"The Chief would like a word with you ma'am" he said to her.

"Okay thanks," she replied, her head starting to thump again. "I'll be there in a few minutes."

* * *

As she sat in his office the Chief said

"It's a good idea putting the victim's picture in the mail, and the photofit of her assailant. We'll release a confidential telephone contact number in the hope we'll get more response. Now I want to organise some security for you. You need to keep a police radio with you at all times."

"I've got my mobile phone, Sir," she told him.

"I'm aware of that Inspector, but you'll get a quicker response from a police radio, and we'll also get a panic button installed in your house, connected through to the station, so we can have someone there in minutes if the need arises, especially if there's a squad car in the area at the time."

She was just about to ask if it was really necessary, when she suddenly stopped herself. Her mind went back to the scene at the first victim's house. She had never come across such a dreadful sight in all her years in the police force. Only a maniac could do that to another human being.

"I'll go along with whatever you suggest, sir," she agreed.

"That's good," he said, smiling.

"Now there's just one other thing I need to discuss, I know this will be awkward, but I'll have to take some manpower off you for another case."

"You can't Sir, I've only got twenty officers on the team and I've already had to cancel holiday leave for two PCs, which I didn't like doing, but I had no choice," she protested.

"I've no choice Inspector, we have what appears to be a domestic murder. It does seem like manslaughter, but we can't be certain. I'll need at least three or four officers from your team. I can appreciate this copycat Ripper case must take priority over all others, but we do need to give some of the available workforce over to this other case."

"But I really can't spare them sir. There are so many more enquiries we need to make in both murder cases."

"I appreciate the size of your enquiry, Inspector. This is one of the biggest murder cases we've ever had, but we've overstretched our budget as it is, so I've no other alternative. As soon as they've finished with the new case, I'll assign them back to you immediately."

Josephine was angry and frustrated, but nevertheless she could see the predicament the Chief was in, so she reluctantly agreed.

* * *

When she arrived home, as she entered her hallway she heard a noise in the kitchen and became alarmed for a few moments. Then she noticed a familiar large yellow rucksack at the bottom of the stairs.

"Is that you Jessica?" she shouted down the hall.

"I'm in the kitchen Mum, making a snack."

Josephine walked down the hall and into the kitchen.

"Snack? Looks more like a six course meal," she remarked, hugging her daughter.

Jessica kissed her on the cheek which surprised Josephine, as she had never been demonstrative, even as a child.

"I wasn't expecting you until next week."

"I've been worried about you Mum."

"There's no need."

"Come off it, I do read the newspapers you know, and Bill told me he was contacting you on your email."

"Bill had no right to tell you that!" Josephine said angrily.

Jessica slammed down the saucepan of beans she was holding.

"Don't you dare have a go at Bill. I'm your daughter and I've a right to know if you're in any danger. He didn't want to tell me all the facts, but I managed to get it out of him. Now promise me you won't say anything to him."

"Alright, if it makes you happy, I won't say a word," Josephine agreed.

"Look Mum, I won't rest easily until this maniac is under lock and key."

Josephine smiled to herself. *'God she sounds like me, when I nag her about staying out late, and not taking care of herself properly. It's like a role reversal,'* she thought.

"It's lovely to see you Jess, and I'm touched by your concern," she told her daughter as she filled the kettle.

"Well, now Dad's gone there's no one else to worry about you," Jessica stated.

About half an hour later they had both consumed beans on toast, followed by bananas, and a creamcake that Jessica had brought home with her. Jessica insisted it was just a snack, but to

Josephine it felt like a positive feast. While she was drinking her coffee, Josephine lit a cigarette and put her feet up on the sofa. She decided to tell Jessica about Andrew Blythe. As she confided to Jessica the progress of their affair she felt as if she was talking to a friend or sister, and mentioned they had slept together.

"What's he like in the sack then, Mum? Was he good?"

"Oh Jessica, you can be so crude at times!"

"What's crude about two adults have satisfying and fulfilling sex? I hope that you and Dad always had a good sex life! You must have missed it. Been frustrated lately?" she teased Josephine, slyly.

"All I'm prepared to say, young lady, is that Andrew is a perfect gentleman; tender, loving, caring and..." She paused deliberately for a moment while Jessica waited in anticipation.

"...Bloody good in bed! And I'll kill you if you ever breathe a word of this to anyone."

They laughed, teased and confided in each other like two close girlfriends for the next hour and Josephine realised that her awkward and rebellious teenager had now become her friend.

* * *

The following day their planned trip to Dartmoor had to be postponed, due to

Josephine's work commitments and Jessica's need to return to University to revise for exams. The short time they had spent together had been good for both of them. As Josephine drove Jessica to the train station, Jessica said

"Now promise me you'll be careful Mum, and if anything's wrong, you'll phone me."

Josephine smiled

"That's exactly what I used to say to you each week. It's history repeating itself... yes, I promise, and you do the same."

The train pulled out of the station, with Jessica leaning out of the window waving. Josephine stopped smiling when the train was no longer in sight. She walked from the station feeling frightened and alone.

Chapter 15

THAT AFTERNOON JOSEPHINE had arranged to meet one of the force's computer experts, DS Michael Dowding. He'd offered to come to the station but she suggested she spoke to him at his office in Exeter. She took the motorway to Exeter and was there in little over an hour. Even though she was leaving the relative peace of Torquay to drive to the hustle and bustle of a city, she felt as if she were escaping to some far-off place. She needed a change of scenery, even if the landscape was just buildings, cars and traffic jams.

When she finally reached the large building that was Exeter Police Headquarters, DS Dowding was waiting for her in reception.

"Did you manage to find a space in the car park?" he asked in a deep Devon drawl.

"Yes, eventually. Unfortunately I'm in a reserved space and I don't have my car-sticker with me," Josephine said.

"Don't worry, I'm sure it will be fine, but you can leave the keys with George on reception – he'll move it for you if necessary."

They went up to his office on the fourth floor and he offered Josephine coffee. She was glad of the refreshment, as the journey down had drained her, despite the fact it hadn't taken long. She hated motorway driving, unless she was in a squad car, when she found that other motorists tended to slow down and drive more carefully. On the way there she had had a lorry driving far too fast behind her. *'If ever I have to brake for any reason he'll go straight into the back of me,'* she'd thought. *'He wouldn't be doing this if I'd been in a police vehicle.'* She'd hoped to come across some motorway police so that she could report him, but she hadn't seen anyone on the motorway. She thought how ironic it was that everyone thought her life might be in danger from the copycat Jack The Ripper, and she could end up getting killed by some maniac driver.

After they had finished their coffee, she explained to Dowding that if their investigation proved fruitless their only hope of catching 'Jack Two', as they'd nicknamed him, would be to try and track him down through the computer.

"Your man is obviously intelligent, and has a wide knowledge of computers. He may not be a programmer, but he's probably at least on the fringes of the computer industry – there still aren't that many people in Britain with expert knowledge of the internet, unless they do work in the industry. He's obviously looked into the best way of disguising the origin of his email, and has settled on using browser-based email as the best way of doing it. It's going to be difficult for us to trace him. We've contacted Hotmail and explained the situation, and in view of it being a murder investigation they're watching the account – but the chances are he won't use it again. He'll have set up a number of accounts, possibly with Hotmail, possibly with other providers."

"David Burke, an expert on serial killers who we've been consulting, said it was a pity that that I couldn't try and send messages back to him. Is there any chance that it would work?"

"I don't think so. To pick up your mail he'd have to access the account. There's a good chance we'd still not get him – he's probably using public facilities such as a library or cybercafé to use the accounts. He may try and contact you to meet on cyberspace 'neutral territory' – by meeting online in a chatroom or posting to a public newsgroup, but the initiative is wholly his," Dowding said, resignedly.

"What's cyberspace? And chatrooms? And

newgroups?"

"Cyberspace is a way of viewing the internet as an analogue of our own world – you exist as Josephine Blake in the real world, with a set of real friends, a real house and so on. In cyberspace you can re-invent yourself to some extent – because no-one can see you, and your friends might very well be in different countries. Your address is your email address, or your web site. Many people construct complex online personalities for themselves, and it can be very addictive. Remember, in cyberspace you can be as powerful as your imagination allows you to be. It looks like our man's inventiveness may have strayed over the boundary into real life.

"A chatroom is very much like email. It's an internet channel that you and a number of other users are logged onto at the same time. When you type a message and transmit it, all the other users logged onto that channel receive the message. Usually it's for net enthusiasts, but it's also used for everything from role playing to games discussions and so on. But, as with everything, one of its main uses is allowing people to engage in mutual sexual fantasies – the 'cybersex' you might have seen in newspaper headlines. One online provider is notorious for chatrooms that feature simulated rape and murder."

"So you think our man might have started off by participating in something like that?"

"It's something to consider. If he started before he'd thought about moving his fantasies into the real world, he might have left a trail out there."

"And what about newsgroups?"

"Newsgroups are public discussion forums that cover everything from arts to science and all points in between. As well as the usual hefty dose of sex. It's estimated that much of the bandwidth of the internet is devoted to spam going to newsgroups."

"Spam? Bandwidth?" Josephine looked startled.

"Because the groups are so specific it's easy to identify what the interests of the members are. They're named with an hierarchical structure – alt. sex. fetish, or rec. arts. music. elvis for example. Alt. sex. fetish is a sub-group of the alt. sex hierarchy, which is in turn a subgroup of the alt. – for alternative – hierarchy. People target the groups to advertise their products with the electronic equivalent of junk mail – spam. It's named after the Monty Python 'spam' sketch. Bandwidth is simply the amount of data that can be carried by the internet. If there's too much spam they become like blocked pipes in a water system. It's as if the Post Office couldn't deliver your mail due to the volume of circulars.

Spammers were some of the people who started the whole anonymous remailing business.

"If there were a way to tell the killer to name a chatroom, or newsgroup for you to contact each other through, it would be safe for him, and you might get an angle on what he's doing, or provoke him into giving away a clue as to his identity."

"Well, if there is any way you can think of we could get him to make contact, please let us know. We've only got until the thirtieth of September before he strikes again, and quite frankly, I'm desperate!"

"I'll try and think of another way – but the obvious way is probably not one you'll like. Use the press to tell him to contact you and specify a method of contact," Dowding suggested.

"I can't think my Chief would thank me for that suggestion, but I take your point. Thank you very much for your time – I'd better go and see if my car's still there," she got up to go.

"It's been a pleasure," he grasped her proffered hand firmly in his. "I hope we meet again under happier circumstances. In the meantime, I'll see if there's any trail I can pick up on the internet."

Chapter 16

JOSEPHINE LOGGED ON to her computer to check her email. Recently she had felt sick and anxious as she did this, wondering what sick and depraved communication would await her. Now, in a strange way, she almost welcomed them. She was painfully aware that the messages were the only weapons she possessed in this strange shadow fight to prevent another terrible and painful death. *'Come on you sick bastard, you're bound to slip up sooner or later and give away something you don't want us to know. And as soon as you do, we'll have you!'*

She inspected the list of new email. Nothing from john@hotmail.com. But a new address scrolled onto her screen as the messages were received – jackdr2@rocketmail.com. Josephine opened the mail.

Hi
You worked it out. I had every faith in you.
The papers are calling me Jack Two.
I wanted my email address to be jacktheripper2 this time – but someone had taken it first. There's some sick bastards out there, eh Josephine?
The next is a double date
But you already know that.
I may send you another clue, if you mend your ways,
I bet you were as beautiful as your daughter in your younger days.
Jack2

"You *BASTARD!*"

Josephine felt numb, frozen and violated. She sat, looking at the words of his message as if there was some secret to be gleaned from them. Bill entered the silent office.

"Can you believe it – my one afternoon off in weeks, I was going to the beach and it's bloody well tipping it down!"

Josephine sat motionless staring at the screen, her breathing laboured.

"And to cap it all there's been a mugging in the High Street – we've caught the little tosser though!"

Josephine still didn't answer.

"Are you alright love?" Bill asked, concerned.

"No... no, I'm not..."

"Jesus! What's wrong, you're as white as a sheet!" Bill asked, inspecting her more closely.

Josephine's face was covered in a fine damp sheen, her breathing was coming in short, fast gasps.

"Wait there – I'm getting the doctor! He's on site at the moment," he ran out of the door.

Josephine knew she was having a panic attack, but felt too weak to fight it. As she started to feel faint she could hear a voice saying *'Don't worry, you're going to be alright.'*

She remembered saying "Get Andrew," before she lost consciousness.

* * *

An hour later she was resting quietly in the doctor's examining room at the station. Andrew was by her side holding her hand. She started to tell him about the message on the computer.

"There's no need to go through that now. We saw the message. Bill has contacted Jessica and she's safe. The Nottingham Police have been alerted and are giving her protection – not that she's that happy about it," he said with a smile, "She reckons it'll cramp her style."

"But she was home two days ago, and he knows about it! He must have been watching my house. Do you think she's in danger?" she asked shakily.

"I think she's quite safe in Nottingham. You remember when we discussed why the murders were done in Torquay, we decided it was because he has local knowledge. He's quite cagey, our killer. He wants to keep close to home."

The police doctor entered the examining room. He was a large bearded Scot, of dour demeanour.

"Feeling better, are we?" he interjected.

"I thought I was having a heart attack," she muttered.

"Just a panic attack, lassie. Bought on by stress and overwork."

Josephine felt ashamed.

"I should have handled it better," she answered.

"Life doesn't provide us with much training for dealing with madmen who threaten our loved ones," said Andrew. "You've good reason to fear this man and you thought your daughter was in danger. You've been bottling your fear up – not just fear for your daughter, or even fear for yourself, but fear for the unknown women who will suffer on the thirtieth if we don't catch him. You must understand though – none of it is your fault, and if you *don't* stop him, any further deaths are at his door only – not yours. Don't take his guilt on yourself. You're a good and loving person – he's the monster."

Josephine wept for a few minutes.

"I'm so ashamed," she said between sobs.

"Why? Just getting divorced is one of the most stressful things that can happen in a person's life. Being the conduit between the police and a serial killer has to be off the scale somewhere! These things need to come out, not be bottled up inside," Andrew said gently.

The doctor took her blood pressure and listened to her heart and lungs.

"Well, there's nothing physically wrong, you'll be pleased to know – you're basically as strong as an Aberdeen Angus. But look at you woman – you're tired out. You need a good twelve hours sleep. I don't believe in them myself, but I can give you some mild hypnotics to help you relax."

"No, I'd rather not. If I get stressed again I'll have a brandy."

"Well, I'm not one to recommend drinking as a solution to life's problems. But a wee dram before bedtime won't hurt you. I'd make it a Scotch, myself."

Josephine looked up at Andrew.

"I'm sure he's watching my every move. I feel I can't go anywhere without security. He's getting closer."

"That's good; he's being more daring, and taking more risks. He's bound to make a mistake, and then we'll get him."

"I'm not sure I can fight him any more,"

Josephine said. "I don't understand him. You're a forensic psychologist Andrew – what does he want? Help me to understand him!"

"He's like a cat that tortures and kills a mouse and then brings it into the house for its owner."

"What do you mean?" Josephine asked.

"I think he feels he has a strange relationship with you and wants to tell you when he kills. He wants your attention – it excites him. That's what the email messages are about. I think Jessica is safe, but you, and those you work with, may very well be in danger."

* * *

Despite Andrew's insistence, he didn't stay the night with Josephine at her house. She slept alone with her police radio, and a panic button beside her. There was a PC stationed outside the house in a squad car. Strangely she didn't feel frightened – it was as if the dam of her fear had broken, and now she could live with it. She slept well, despite the recent trauma.

The following morning found her, post-shower, in the kitchen making coffee and toast for herself and the somewhat stiff and tired PC.

"When are you off duty?" she asked him.

"I'm changing shifts at eight-thirty ma'am. Another officer will be here to relieve me."

Josephine looked at the kitchen clock. It was twenty past seven.

"Only I need some fresh air, so I'm going for a walk along the beach."

"I'll have to tag along ma'am – Chief's orders."

"That's OK, be my guest."

As she walked along the beach in her tracksuit and trainers the PC walked a few yards behind to give her some privacy. The sun was just breaking through the clouds and the sea was calm and clear, like a sheet of blue glass.

Josephine always retreated to the beach when she was down – she found it therapeutic. It was the time only she really felt at peace. The bigness of the sea was reassuring somehow, as if it could swallow all mankind's problems and still have room for more. She reached the rocks at the far end of the beach and sat on one and looked out to sea. She felt stronger, and more determined not to let the killer get the better of her. She knew it was a battle of wits between them, and that she was dealing with a dangerous madman, who she thought was unstable but highly intelligent.

A few months previously she couldn't have been so resolute and strong willed. Tom leaving her to live with another woman had reduced her confidence to its lowest ebb. Now she realised that she had good friends who she could call any time she felt the need to talk. Her new closeness to Jessica had provided her with a wellspring of strength, and her relationship with Andrew had restored her confidence, both in her attractiveness and her ability to move on and form new relationships. Her heart skipped a beat as she thought of him. *'I don't know how long it will last between us, maybe he won't be the great love affair, but he's kind and he cares and at this moment in time I've never needed anyone like I need him,'* she reflected dreamily as she watched the still blue ocean.

Her thoughts were suddenly interrupted by the sound of the PC's voice.

"I think we should be heading back ma'am – if my relief finds us gone he may fear the worst."

"Of course – I'm sorry I've dragged you all this way," she said, smiling.

"I've enjoyed it ma'am, it's not often I get on the beach."

They set back to the house at a brisk pace.

* * *

Andrew called about half an hour after Josephine arrived at the station.

"How are you this morning?" he asked.

"Much, much better Andrew. I slept well, and have had breakfast with a handsome young PC. And afterwards, a morning stroll by the sea together," she teased.

"Stop it, I'm getting jealous. You should have let me stay – I'd have made the breakfast."

"I needed a good night's sleep, my love, and I certainly wouldn't have achieved that if you *had* stayed!"

"Enough! *Mea Culpa!*"

"I've got someone standing by my terminal if I'm out of the station, so they can contact me the moment I receive another email – although his messages have hardly been frequent."

"Yes, but Josephine, he may be beginning the fugue state that serial killers often enter. Don't forget, if he's following the original murders he's only got two more dates he can kill on. Statistically serial killers tend to accelerate their activities as time goes on – as if inviting discovery. Because he has to stick to the original dates he can't increase the rate at which he kills, leaving him only one outlet for the increasing tension – his communications with you!"

"I'm wondering if Michael Dowding's suggestion – that we should try and use the media to set up some kind of meeting in cyberspace – would be a good idea?"

"We should contact David Burke as well, and see if he has anything to suggest – anything that might encourage him to contact you. I'll speak to him and see if he can come up with anything."

"I'll leave it up to you, Andrew. I'm all out of

ideas – I'll go along with anything he suggests. I've got to run, I've got a debriefing."

"I'll see you this evening – and I'm not taking no for an answer!"

"OK, but we're going out. I can't face cooking at the moment," she told him.

"*I* shall prepare dinner," he replied as he rang off.

Chapter 17

TWO DAYS LATER, a recent photograph of Sheila Jones and a photofit of the man the Torquay Police were looking for were shown as part of an appeal for help on national television. The only reply was from a Jackie Burton, who phoned the confidential number given out on the show.

She came, rather reluctantly, into Torquay Police Station for questioning, pleasure at the excitement of contributing to a high-profile murder investigation battling with annoyance at having to use half a day's holiday to do it. Josephine had suggested that they could visit her at home in an ordinary car, but she seemed reluctant to involve the police in her family life.

On the evening of the eighth of September she had been for a drink and a meal with some friends from work and was walking through Torquay town centre, towards the car-park to recover her car. She was ninety percent certain that she had seen Sheila Jones with a man walking towards the same car park. She couldn't give a good description of the man, or even whether he was similar to the photofit picture she'd been shown. The photofit wasn't the most reliable picture anyway – the doorman at the Black Cat had not been able to give a clear description of him. He'd never really had a good look at his face, something which Josephine thought, like the nondescript clothing, was wholly intentional on the part of the killer.

Josephine and Bill introduced themselves to her and then they showed her into the interview room. Josephine sat down and Bill offered her a seat at the other side of the table and then sat down himself. She was a slightly built woman in her twenties with short red hair – cropped in a modern style, it gave her an impish look that suited her small pointed face.

To begin with Jackie was a little anxious – understandable if the man she had seen was the Jack The Ripper killer – but they assured her that her identity would remain a secret, and no-one except the team working on the case would be given any information about her.

"Thank you for contacting us Ms Burton," Josephine began, "We need all the help we can get, but let me assure you your statement is strictly confidential and no details of this conversation will be disclosed to the media."

"That's reassuring," she replied.

"Now, you say you're more or less certain that the woman you saw was Sheila Jones?"

"Oh yes. I remember her, because she seemed too old to be wearing the clubwear she'd was dressed in. I'm sorry, it sounds terrible now, but I remember thinking 'there's mutton dressed as lamb'. She had a lilac top, those tight pants they wear at dance clubs and white trainers, and was carrying a white sports bag. She looked very fit – it was her face that looked old. That's why it stayed in my mind – old face, young body."

"That's fine. Now, can you remember anything about the man she was with?"

"No, I'm afraid I don't. He was walking in the shadows at the other side of her – she blocked my view of him. I remember thinking that their conversation was a bit one sided. She talked to him, but his responses were just grunts, really. All I can say is that he was the same general build and colouring of the man in the photofit picture, but as I didn't see his face I couldn't swear it was him."

"Can you remember if they seemed friendly, like they knew one another?"

"As I said the conversation seemed one sided to me. I thought he'd picked her up for a one night stand, and she was trying to make more of it. I wouldn't say they were intimate – not a couple so to speak. Perhaps friends or acquaintances – but not very good ones."

"So there was no aggression between them, and he wasn't using any force against her?" Bill said.

"No – I got the picture she was rather pleased with her catch, the way she was rabbiting on to him."

"So you walked past them?"

"Yes, they were about half way down the High Street, on the small slope by the public toilets."

"Were they standing by, or about to get into a car, can you recall?"

"I don't think so. I can't remember a car being parked nearby. I just assumed that they were heading for the same car park as me – most people in town at that time are, the clubs and pubs have chucked out. But to be honest I just didn't notice."

"Well, thank you for your help, if you can think of anything else please phone me on my mobile. Then you won't have to leave a message with anyone at the station, it'll be more private." As she said this Josephine handed her a card with the number on.

"It's hard to believe that the man I saw could be responsible for her murder – he seemed so ordinary," she remarked.

"Most of them do, that's why they're so difficult to catch," Josephine replied.

* * *

Josephine and Bill sat in the staff canteen, eating strawberry doughnuts and drinking tea.

"These are nice. It makes a change for them to have any decent cakes in, they're normally dry or stale," Bill remarked, as he wiped a smear of jam from his chin.

"Mmm, they are nice, I shouldn't really, but still… Josephine said as she took another cake from the plate in front of her.

"Do you think Sheila Jones had just met him that evening?" Bill asked.

"No, I don't. According to her husband they were happily married and she was devoted to him and their child," Josephine told him.

"Yes, but was he right in his assumption? I mean, you women can pull the wool over our eyes. Maybe she'd been having an affair with someone behind his back?"

"Oh Bill! Sometimes you can be such a chauvinist. I, for one, don't believe she'd be that relaxed or friendly with someone she'd just met. I don't think she was having a relationship with him, but I think she may have known him beforehand. Perhaps he was just an acquaintance."

"So if he'd offered her a lift home, she'd have accepted it if she trusted him," Bill added. "Jane Fielding invited the same man into her house and had sex with him, so she must also have trusted him."

"I think he must have a split personality; one side of the man is a monster! He's sadistic and inflicts terrible injuries on his victims before finally killing them. But there's also a side which is friendly, attractive and apparently trustworthy. Do you remember what David Burke said at the meeting? He could be your friend, brother or neighbour."

"I've just had a disturbing thought," Bill said, as he finished off his coffee.

"What's that?" Josephine asked.

"*You* could already know this man – perhaps he's a friend!" he suggested.

"That's rubbish! I'd be able to tell – I'm a good judge of character. I can always tell when someone's genuine or not."

"That would be women's intuition rearing its head again, would it?" Bill remarked sarcastically.

"Don't knock it until you've tried it – it works for me. I've never met this copycat Jack The Ripper, but believe me, if I had, I'd know it!" Her voice was confident and certain, and revealed little of the turmoil Bill's remark had thrown her into.

Chapter 18

ROGER GRAHAM, one of the world's leading experts on Jack The Ripper, sat in Josephine's office. She had told him two days previously she could have travelled to London to consult with him, but he knew time was running out, and that she hadn't much to spare. Since he was now semi-retired he agreed to come Devon to liaise with her again as he had done a week earlier at the Superintendent's meeting.

He began.

"Despite the fact the killer is obsessed with Jack The Ripper and regards him as some sort of hero, he can't possibly know the identity of the original Ripper – that's eluded the top detectives of the century. It would be impossible to copy Jack's crimes exactly. He's just trying to be similar to him, and is taking the bits of the original crimes he likes and ignoring the rest. He's changed some of the modus operandi for a start – the original Ripper almost certainly performed most of his mutilations after death." He paused for a moment looking through the papers in front of him. "Having said that," he continued, "Concerning his second victim, there are certain similarities between Sheila Jones and the Ripper's second victim, Annie Chapman. They were both dark-haired plump women."

"I suppose," Josephine intervened "that could be either coincidence or he may have been purposely looking for someone who was similar. It seems that she may have known her assailant slightly."

Graham continued:

"We now believe, from thorough investigation and research over thc years, that the probable reason The Ripper killed two women on the 30th September was because he had been interrupted in the post-mortem mutilation of his first victim on that date, Elizabeth Stride. Her throat had been cut from ear to ear and she had lost nearly all her life's blood, but there had been no other knife marks, or removal of organs, like the previous victims.

"I think he may have not got the morbid satisfaction he normally derived from his crimes and, unfulfilled, murdered a second victim on the same day – Catherine Eddowes, known as Kate.

The most reliable timings put this second murder within an hour of the killing of Elizabeth Stride. On this occasion he wasn't disturbed. Her stomach had been laid open, and he left all his usual, obscene trade marks.

"So it may be that your man will commit only one crime, but it is impossible to predict."

"I've spent a great deal of time studying your notes and researching the Ripper killings myself. I came across the message that was written in chalk on a wall in Goulston Street just after the killing of Catherine Eddowes – 'THE JUWES ARE NOT THE MEN THAT WILL BE BLAMED FOR NOTHING.' Nearby, a piece of the victim's apron was found covered in blood," Josephine told him.

"That's correct. It was never really known if The Ripper wrote those words, or some practical joker."

"The Ripper's victims were all prostitutes and yet our victims were respectable women. However our killer may have thought them to be 'loose women' – Jane Fielding slept with him so he could have formed that impression of her, and Sheila Jones was friendly with him – perhaps too friendly? He could have thought she was leading him on, I suppose the experts could put this better, but do you see my point?"

"Yes. All the Ripper's victims were prostitutes,

so he obviously had an aversion to them. This man may or may not feel the same. I'm no psychologist, but I don't think he'll stop until he's killed five. This is his goal. The ultimate challenge."

"The way I feel at the moment, if we don't catch him I'll hand in my resignation," Josephine stated.

* * *

"Look, I know things are a bit stressed at the moment, with some of the lads having to cancel their holiday leave, and the Chief going on about our budget. I know all this security is getting you down, and you're a bit uptight and nervous..." Bill prattled on.

"Get to the point Bill, It's not like you to go round the Wrekin."

"Uh... well, it's my birthday on Friday."

He sounded like a nervous school boy.

"Oh yes, of course – I'd forgotten all about it."

"Well that's understandable, with what you've been though lately, and I know you haven't felt well..."

"You're doing it again Bill..." she interrupted him.

"Am I?" He suddenly became decisive and said "I'm going to have a bit of a do at my flat, I know it's a bad time..."

"I think it's a marvellous idea, Bill. Just what I need to take my mind off this case, if only for a few hours."

"Right, I'm glad you think so. I've checked the staff rotas, and a few people are off that day, there's plenty of beer and lager for the men, and I could get some wine for the girls..."

"Oh that's kind of you to think of us, one bottle between six girls," she said teasingly.

"It's actually preparing the food, that I'm a bit worried about."

"I'll make you some sandwiches and quiches, with a few dips and nibbles."

He looked relieved.

"Well that's great, if it's not too much trouble."

"If it was I wouldn't have offered. It'll do me good, not that I haven't got enough on, but I can't remember the last time I prepared a buffet. I'll enjoy doing it."

"Right, that's settled then," Bill said relieved.

"Can I bring a friend?" Josephine asked.

"Yes, providing she's well endowed and under forty," Bill grinned.

"I was thinking of a male friend."

"Not bloody Andrew Blythe! He's a bit of a bore – he'll be talking shop all night."

"On the contrary, he's a very attractive and exciting man, when you get to know him."

"Well he's not *my* type!"

"I should hope not. By the way is Joyce coming?"

"Well... I'm not sure," he sounded vague.

"You *have* asked her I hope."

"No... er, not yet."

"You'd better ring her now, because if she finds out you've had a birthday party and not invited her she won't be too pleased."

"How would she find out?"

Josephine remained silent and just smiled slyly at him He tutted in defeat as he picked up the phone and dialled.

"Oh, hello, is your Mum there..."

* * *

Josephine had worked with Chief Inspector Martin Johnson when she'd first joined the force in the Midlands some years previously. He was a Detective Sergeant in those days and she was a young constable. They hadn't kept in regular touch since she'd moved to Devon, and he was now with the Metropolitan Police in London, although she had contacted him three years previously to ask for his help when one of her murder suspects had been sighted in London.

He'd recently been working on a case that was similar to the murders that were being committed on Josephine's patch and the body was actually found in what had been the old Whitechapel area of London. Josephine wondered if the two crimes could be connected in any way. She had found his current office via cross-force inquiries. For the first five minutes of their telephone conversation they reminisced about the past, and asked after certain colleagues that they'd both worked with.

"Have you still got those bright blue eyes?" Johnson asked her.

"Well they're still there, not so bright as they were in those days, just a lot more lined," she replied truthfully.

"So you've got your hands full at the moment, possibly one of the biggest cases you've had in your area for years I'd say."

"It's not only the big cities that get the crime you know," she replied.

"But seriously, Josephine, I hear the killer has been contacting you by email, about his crimes."

"That's right."

"Well then I hope you're being careful, and have the right protection."

"Yes, I've got everything I need – panic buttons, alarms, the lot. But I didn't want them."

"You were always stubborn as a girl – I see you haven't lost the trait," he joked. "Anyway, to get back to business," he continued in a serious voice. "I've studied the files and papers you've sent me, and I'm sure the man we're after is not the same as your assailant. He did strangle his victim, an eighteen year old prostitute and then stabbed, her but only once – she wasn't mutilated like your two victims. It's just that in London, so many people are so obsessed with Jack The Ripper they tend to link any similar crimes. Do you know there's even a magazine published about him that comes out every three months? Which is incredible when you think his crimes are over a century old! It's even been said that if you draw a line between the locations where his victims were found they make some sort of magical symbol.

"But to get back to our victim, Kelly Ryan. I checked the forensic report and there were no similar carpet fibres found on her body as with your two victims, and furthermore the description of the man seen in the vicinity does not match the description of your suspect. We obviously have not solved the crime and the case is still open, so there's always a possibility they could be connected, but it's highly unlikely In fact we're following a lead at the moment in which we think an old boyfriend of Kelly Ryan's may be involved in her murder. If anything comes to light that I think may help your case I'll contact you."

"Thanks Martin, that would be appreciated."

"Anyway when this case is over, you'll have to come down to London and I'll show you the sights," he told her.

"That would be great, but the way I feel at the moment I think I'll be working on this case for the rest of my life!"

"I know the feeling, still, chin up Josephine, I'm sure you'll crack it," he said finally, before he hung up.

Chapter 19

THERE WAS A BRIEFING in the incident room on the Friday afternoon before Bill's birthday party

"Now I know those of you that are off duty this evening will have the Sergeant's booze-up on your mind," she joked, "But we need to go over what we have so far, so if I could have everyone's attention? Two victims so far, Jane Fielding and Sheila Jones; we think both victims knew and possibly even trusted their assailant. We have two sightings of the murderer in the first case. Jane Fielding's neighbour, Sue Proctor and the doorman at the Black Cat nightclub. In Sheila Jones' case, we have a statement from Ms Jackie Burton, who saw her talking to a man in the High Street shortly after she had left her friends. We believe this man to be her assailant. You all have details of the email messages I have received from the killer. I've checked with cross-force enquiries about the murder committed in London, but at this moment in time there's nothing to suggest the crimes are linked. What's the position about the list of members from the Harbour Fitness Club?" she asked.

"No luck up to now I'm afraid ma'am, but we're still going through them," one DC said.

"Well get a move on. I want every person who's a member checked out by Monday. How's it going with the carpet outlets Bill?"

"The report's completed on all employers and it's proved fruitless" he replied

"I've got a computer expert based at HQ at Exeter who's trying to track down where the email messages are being sent from, and I'm still liaising with Roger Graham as to where the killer may strike again. Does any one have anything to report?"

No-one had, much to Josephine's disappointment.

"Right, you'll all be pleased to know that's all for now, enjoy the party everyone, because next week I want one hundred percent from you all, until this man's caught!"

* * *

"Great party, Sarge," one young PC said a little drunkenly, holding a can of lager in one hand and a sandwich in the other.

"I thought that girlfriend of yours was coming, what's her name, Joan?" DC Barnes said to Bill.

"It's Joyce. She may be here later. Still there's no hurry. I mean just look at those two friends Sally's brought with her, they're bloody gorgeous."

They looked over at DC Sally James who was chatting to two girls. Both were tall and slim, and one had long red hair tied in a ponytail while the other had a short blonde bob.

"Mmm, not bad," Barnes commented.

"Not bad! They're bloody stunning. The trouble is I wonder if they think I'm too old for them. Still, he who dares..."

Bill walked over to them with two glasses of wine

"Here we are girls, can't see you with empty glasses, can we? Now then Sally I don't believe you've introduced me to your friends."

Sometime later, Josephine arrived. She wore a black silk knee length mandarin dress and a red jacket.

"You look nice, ma'am" DC Roger Barnes told her.

"I look like everyone's mother! Is there anyone here my age, apart from Bill?" she asked.

Just then Bill came over to her.

"Everyone's enjoying your food, they keep

asking me if I've had the caterers in."

"That's good, at least it'll all get eaten," Josephine replied.

"Can I get you a drink?" he asked.

"Don't bother, I'll help myself. In the kitchen is it?"

"Yes, go through," he told her.

Bill had a one bedroom bachelor flat that was surprisingly tastefully furnished. The large lounge led out into a compact fitted kitchen.

"Not a lot of room in here I'm afraid," Bill said as Josephine poured herself a large glass of white wine.

"By the way, where's your date? I though he'd have come with you."

"Andrew said he'd call in later, as he had an important meeting to attend."

"At this time of night?" Bill asked doubtfully.

"He can be called to cases at the psychiatric hospital at any time of the day or night." She was about to say something else to Bill in Andrew's defence, when someone asked her for a dance.

By two thirty the following morning the last few people were leaving the party. Bill was surprisingly quite sober. He had at one stage earlier been chatting up a friend of Sally's who he thought he might stand a chance with, when Joyce, the woman he'd been dating for the last six months arrived. She had told Bill before the party that she wasn't sure that she'd be able to make it, as she had been having problems with her teenage son, and secretly Bill was hoping she wouldn't come. However she did, and nagged him all night that he was old enough to be the girl's father and what the hell did he think he was playing at. He had managed to get away from Joyce at one point and had said to Josephine

"My God she's worse than my ex-wife. I can't do a bloody thing."

"Well if you want to play around and you don't feel ready to settle down, then I think it's only fair you tell Joyce, and stop messing her around," Josephine had advised him.

When Josephine's taxi arrived to take her home Barnes asked

"Will you be okay ma'am?"

"Yes fine, thanks Barnes. It's the firm I often use, and there will be a PC waiting outside my house when I arrive home. He's probably been there for hours. I shall have to ask him in for a drink."

"Not alcohol I hope ma'am, while he's on duty."

"Don't worry Barnes I'll do him some cocoa."

"I think the reason Andrew Blythe didn't turn up is because he thinks he's too good to socialise with us," Bill commented.

"Don't be ridiculous Bill – he probably just got

held up. Anyway if anyone should be angry, it ought to be me, I've been the lonely wallflower all night" she replied.

"Come off it, I've seen you being chatted up by two different men," he said playfully

Bill looked around the lounge, there were empty cans, paper plates, and bits of food all over the carpet.

"I suppose I'll have to get the carpet cleaned now. What a bloody mess!"

Josephine was just about to go out of the door when she stopped and turned.

"That's *it* Bill!" she exclaimed.

"What?" he asked confused.

"He could be a carpet cleaner – that way he'd have fibres on him from all the different houses he'd visited."

"But wouldn't he wear overalls?" Barnes suggested.

"Yes, but during the day the fibres would come off his overall and onto the seat of his car, and then if he went out in his own clothes they'd attach themselves again. I really think we may have something here, we'll go through it in the morning."

Chapter 20

When she arrived home she spoke to the PC who was sitting in the squad car outside her house. She hadn't met him before, as there was a different officer on duty for each shift. She asked him if he'd like something to eat and drink.

"Well if it's no trouble ma'am, only it's very late," he said as he looked at his watch.

"It's the least I can do. I feel awful you having to sit out here in the car all night. You're welcome to come into the lounge and watch the TV, while I go to bed."

"The Chief's orders are that I stay outside, in case anyone suspicious is seen hanging about. Although I do get out of the car from time to time to stretch my legs, and check around the back of the house and the garden. I've had worse jobs, ma'am and the important thing is your safety."

"Well, at least come in for a while," Josephine

suggested. He agreed and while he sat in the lounge she made him a plate of ham sandwiches and a mug of coffee.

"By the way, how did the Sarge's party go?"

"It was a good night, we've left his flat in a bit of a mess though; still, now he's a bachelor boy again he's got no-one to nag him," she joked

After he had finished his food, the PC stood up.

"Thanks ma'am, that will tide me over till morning. I'd better go back to the car now and radio into the station, to let them know that everything's okay."

He went out of the front door and Josephine locked it behind him.

Before she went to bed, she pressed the button on her telephone answering machine to see if there were any messages for her. She couldn't understand why Andrew hadn't phoned her. She knew he was probably tied up with work, as he had often told her he was called out in the middle of the night to see psychiatric patients when the case was urgent, but she thought he could have given her a quick call, to let her know he couldn't make it to the party.

When she finally got to bed she was tired, but couldn't settle as she felt restless. She did eventually drift off into a sort of semi-conscious sleep, but kept seeing images in her mind of the

Ripper coming towards her with a knife, laughing. Finally she did manage to drop off and had been asleep for about an hour when the phone at the side of her bed started to ring. She jumped up suddenly, and her head started to spin. As she picked up the receiver, she looked at the time on her radio alarm, it was just after five o'clock.

"Is that you Andrew, where have you been?" she said croakily.

"Inspector Blake, is that you?"

"Yes," she replied.

"It's Sergeant Bryan here."

"Oh! What is it Sergeant?"

"I'm afraid he's struck again, we've found another body." Her heart started to pound in her chest. "What! He can't! It's impossible. What's the date?"

"It's the twenty-fourth today, ma'am," the Sergeant replied.

"But he's six days early, it can't be him!" She felt in a state of confused panic and disbelief.

"What's the address?" she asked.

"It's Lancome Road, Brixham; do you want us to send a car?"

"Uhh... no, it's okay, there's a squad car outside, I'll get him to take me. I'll be there as soon as I can."

'I need some coffee to wake me up,' she thought as she headed for the kitchen. While the kettle was

boiling she pulled on a pair of jeans and a sweater. and went outside to the PC in the car.

He got out.

"Are you alright ma'am, what's wrong?" he said, concerned.

"Don't worry, I'm fine. I've just had a call that there's been another murder. I've told them we'll go in your car."

"Yes, of course ma'am. I'll radio in to the station to let them know," he told her.

"I won't be long. I'm just going to grab a coffee before we go."

Ten minutes later they were speeding out of Torquay towards Brixham. The police car didn't have its siren or blue flashing light on, as the roads were almost deserted. The police officer drove up to the harbour at Brixham and passed where the Golden Hind stood. Josephine only visited Brixham Harbour during the day, when it was a bustling fishing port, full of noisy seagulls. The boats at the far end would be laden with fishing nets, and along one side of the harbour, men stood in small brightly painted kiosks, trying to persuade holiday makers to book boat trips with them. On fine days local artists would display their paintings at the far end of the harbour and in the high season there would be portrait artists and people would queue to have their picture drawn in pastels.

The scene was totally different in the early hours of the morning. The place looked deserted and bare, despite the fact the harbour was full of boats.

The police car sped around the square and turned left into a side street. The road was narrow and had quaint fisherman's cottages on either side. When they reached the far end, Josephine could see blue flashing lights and the tape cordoning off the crime scene, lit in garish amber by a large Victorian street lamp. An officer was logging the various members of the force as they arrived.

Bill, the police surgeon, and three other officers were already at the scene when Josephine arrived. Josephine walked up to where the body lay and was about six foot or so away when Bill said

"You can't go too close, ma'am until we've got the gear on. The SOCO team will be here soon with the suits"

"God, what am I thinking of?" Josephine replied.

"Well if you're anything like me, you've got a terrible hangover. Mind you I'd only been in bed a couple of hours when they rang me. I was supposed to be off duty today, so I could have a lie-in after the party."

Josephine wasn't paying any attention to Bill as she looked over at the body. At first she couldn't see the victim, as the police surgeon was bending over the body. As he stood to one side for a moment. the first thing Josephine noticed was a mass of blonde hair, which was enhanced by light from the street lamp. The victim's clothes were so saturated in blood, it was difficult to determine their original colour and style.

The police surgeon spoke to her.

"Her windpipe has been severed. She wouldn't have been able to scream for help. Also the main artery in the neck was cut – she'd have bled to death in a matter of minutes. I can't see any other stab wounds on the body, but when the forensic pathologist arrives he'll be able to tell you more."

Josephine recalled her recent meeting with Roger Graham, when they had discussed Jack The Ripper's third victim. Her throat had been cut, but apart from that there were no other injuries, and this murder appeared to be the same in many respects, apart from the date.

She looked down at the girl again. *'My God she looks younger than my daughter! What in the name of heaven was she doing here at this time of the morning. Perhaps she was murdered somewhere else and left here.'*

"Any idea of time of death?" she asked him.

"Her body was still fairly warm when I arrived. I'd say she had been dead no longer than an hour, and that she was murdered on this very spot," he told her.

"If we could only have caught him before now, this poor girl's life would have been saved. I think it's time I retired, if I can't stop this bloody monster!"

A few minutes later Brian Morrison arrived with the SOCO team. They gave Josephine and Bill protective clothing to wear, and paper shoes to put on, so they could get a closer look at the body without disturbing any evidence. After he'd examined the body, Morrison turned to Josephine and said,

"I agree with what the police surgeon told you – she hasn't been dead very long. See all this blood on the lamp post? I think she put her hand to her neck and then reached out and touched the post as she was dying. Obviously I need to examine the body in greater detail, but I'd say she was murdered on this very spot."

"Well, he's getting more like the Ripper in that respect. This is the first victim he's actually killed on the street, whereas the first one was murdered in her own bed and although we don't know where Sheila Jones was before he dumped her body at the back of the barber's shop, we think he could have killed her in his own home."

When he'd finished his initial examination Morrison tied plastic bags on the young girl's head, hands, and feet to protect them before she was placed in the body bag.

"I don't suppose there's any doubt it's the same man?" Bill asked.

"Oh it's him alright, believe me. The only puzzling thing is, why has he killed her six days too early? By the way, who found the body?" Josephine asked.

"A young couple coming home from a night out. They're sitting over there in a police car."

Josephine looked round at the rows of cottages "Surely someone must've seen something?"

"As her throat was cut so she couldn't scream, and taking into consideration it was about four o'clock in the morning when she died, there was probably no-one about," Bill remarked

"No, I suppose you're right. Mind you, he's getting more daring, killing his victims on the streets."

"I'll make sure her body is taped thoroughly, and I'll get the tapes over to the path lab in the hope that they can detect any fibres. When I've examined her in greater detail I'll contact you straight away," Morrison told Josephine.

"Right, thanks Brian; it's getting out of hand now – three dead and there's no saying how long this slaughter will go on for."

He was just about to answer, when a PC came running over to them.

"We've found a handbag, lying in the road

about fifty yards away. The contents are spilled all over the road – it looks as if it may belong to the victim, ma'am."

"Great – perhaps we'll get an ID from it," Josephine said.

The contents and handbag were checked before they were placed into a clear plastic bag.

Josephine turned to Bill.

"Let's go and speak to the young couple in the squad car, and afterwards I want you to arrange a house-to-house enquiry."

When she got into the police car, the two young people identified themselves as Jamie Caldicott and Sally Heyham. They were both understandably shocked and nervous, having found the badly mutilated body of the young girl. They had been to the Red Lion pub in Brixham for the evening and then afterwards went on to a friend's birthday party. They were both students, and quite hard up, so they decided to walk home from the party, even though it was over four miles. They said that they had first seen the girl lying under the light from about one hundred yards away, and to start with had thought she was drunk. It wasn't until they got closer to her, and saw all the blood, that they realised she had been attacked. The boy had knocked on the doors of several cottages before anyone answered. This was understandable, as the majority of them were occupied by pensioners who were reluctant to answer the door in the middle of the night. When they had spoken to Josephine and Bill, a car took them home. The girl lived with her parents, and the boy in a large house converted into bedsits for students. They were told they needed to come into the station the following day to sign a formal statement.

As Josephine got out of the car, a crowd of people had gathered around the scene, most of whom appeared to be elderly, although that didn't deter them from asking questions and generally being a nuisance. Josephine turned to one PC.

"Get this crowd out of the way. Tell them all to go back inside their houses."

Suddenly one old man pushed his way to the front and shouted,

"It's The Ripper! He's struck again! What I want to know is when are you lot bloody well going to do something about him? It's not safe for us old people to sleep in our beds at night! I pay your wages out of my taxes, and I think it's an absolute disgrace!"

Unfortunately, someone had notified the press, and they arrived on the scene just as the old man was ranting and raving. One reporter seized the opportunity to talk to him.

Josephine turned to Brian Morrison as the body

was being carried away

"This won't do our reputation any good, the press will have a field day with this one. I wonder, if that man *had* heard her screams, if he'd have come to her aid?"

"I very much doubt it," Morrison replied.

Josephine and Bill got into the police car and drove away.

* * *

It was about seven o'clock by the time they arrived back at the station. Josephine decided not to go home and change.

"I don't know about you, but I'm starving," Bill announced. So they both went to the canteen.

As he tucked into a large fry-up, Josephine drank black coffee.

"I don't know how you can eat that after what's just happened," she told him.

"Your problem is, you don't eat enough. You've had no sleep, and you'll be working here till God knows what time tonight. That coffee won't keep you going."

"I suppose you're right, I'll grab something later," Josephine replied. Just then Roger Barnes and Sally James joined them.

"Has anyone reported a missing person yet?" Josephine asked them.

"No ma'am, nothing up till now," Barnes replied.

"I would've thought by now that perhaps the girl's parents would have contacted the police, assuming she lives at home."

"Many youngsters stay at friends' houses and go straight to work or college the next day. Often their parents don't see them sometimes for a day or so. Perhaps if she does live at home, they weren't expecting her back, so they might not be worried," Sally suggested.

"Mmm… I suppose that's feasible," Josephine replied.

"Maybe someone will contact us later, if she doesn't turn up at her workplace or college. Possibly a flatmate might be expecting her to come home."

"There's always the possibility she lives alone," Bill suggested as he mopped up his egg with a slice of bread.

"I suppose we'll have to just wait and see what happens," Josephine said. As she watched Bill tuck into his breakfast she began to feel a bit peckish, so she went to get herself two slices of toast, and a small jar of marmalade from the breakfast bar. She ate one slice, but couldn't manage the second.

"Shame to let that go to waste," Bill said as he picked up the slice and spread it thickly with marmalade.

"You're a human dustbin. Do you know that Bill?" Josephine joked.

"I'll soon work this lot off," he stated.

"What, sitting at a desk all day? I doubt it! Anyway I've wasted enough time I must get back to the office. I'll see you there in five minutes." She got up and walked out of the canteen.

* * *

As Josephine sat at her desk, she turned on the computer to see if there were any email messages for her. The murderer had communicated with her again.

I fooled you – I was early.
You expected it to be on the 30th
Jack would have been so proud. I finished
her off in the street under the lamplight.
Jack.

That was the only message, but to her unease there was file attached to the email a graphics file, kidney.jpg. She double-clicked on the file with her mouse to view it. Slowly her screen filled with an image of the dead girl's body, soaked in blood.

"*Jesus!* You sick bastard!" she shouted out loud

just as Bill walked into the office. He thought for a moment she was referring to him. As he looked at the screen he blanched in horror.

"He must have taken this – but how would he get it developed? He couldn't take it into a photo shop," Bill remarked.

"No, to turn it round this fast he must have a digital camera – even if he had a home darkroom he'd hardly have time to develop, print and scan the film by now," Josephine suggested.

"It proves that, as we suspected, he's heavily into technology. It just gets worse, doesn't it?" Bill said depressingly.

"He's not content just sending messages now, he wants to show me his gruesome work," Josephine uttered. Her heart pounded and she felt another panic attack coming on. She had to use every bit of self control and willpower she could muster in order to get the terrible picture out of her mind, and change the subject.

"It's consistent though. He's called it 'kidney.jpg'. It's thought that the original Ripper sent part of a kidney from one of his victims to George Lusk – the head of the Mile End Vigilance Committee. The Ripper claimed to have eaten the rest of it."

"Christ! I could have done without hearing that after a fry-up!"

"Anyway Bill, before we get down to work,

thanks for the party. It's a pity Andrew didn't turn up. I haven't even heard from him – I must ring him later."

"Yes... It was good, apart from Joyce getting jealous. I haven't had chance to clean up yet."

"Going back to my idea that our killer could possibly be a carpet cleaner, the more I think about it the more it makes sense. As I said to you before even if he wore overalls the fibres would attach themselves to his car seat. Say, for example, he wore a jacket to go out in the evening. If he got into the same vehicle he had driven during the day the fibres would attach themselves to his clothes. Even if he vacuumed his car daily, which is unlikely, he wouldn't be able to remove all the fibres. In fact I don't think for one minute he'd realise he was carrying so many on his clothes. I know it's a long shot, but it's one possible explanation."

"I know it's all supposition at the moment, but it does seem to make sense," Bill said thoughtfully.

"Anyway there's a briefing in the incident room in the next half an hour. We'll get a team to check all the carpet and upholstery cleaners in the area."

* * *

Josephine pinned the photo of the unidentified girl's body on the board next pictures of the other two victims. It was a gruesome sight. There were about fifteen officers in the incident room as Josephine began her briefing.

"Number three, and we don't seem any closer to catching him. We were all expecting the next murder to be on the thirtieth of September, but he's been premature with this one."

"I don't suppose there's any doubt it is him ma'am?" one officer said.

"None whatsoever, in fact he's sent me an email message with a photo of the body attached," she told them.

"Good God," someone uttered.

"We think he used a digital camera at the scene of the crime, and downloaded the image onto his computer. That way there'd be no need for him to get the photo developed through the normal channels. We know the killer is expert with computers – that's why our computer people haven't been able to trace his email address. This does confirm the picture of him that's emerging. The one hopeful point about this is the time of the email. It was sent out of working hours, which means that unless he has access to out-of-hours premises he's had to send it via his own computer," Josephine told them. "I've passed the address details onto our guys and they're going to see what they can do.

"The first two victims were not killed in the

streets, so he's becoming more daring. The original Ripper murdered and disembowelled his victims on the streets, so now our killer wants to do the same. Have there been any new reports of missing persons?" she asked

"No ma'am," one officer replied. "We've also checked all the other stations in the surrounding areas, with no luck."

"We'll give it a few more hours and then her picture will have to be put in the newspaper. Unfortunately she was wearing no jewellery and carried nothing on her person that would give us even the slightest clue to her identity, or anything that would identify her was removed by the killer. Her handbag contained just a comb and loose change. There were no credit cards or anything else that would identify her," Bill told the team.

"As you know, we've been making enquiries at carpet shops and warehouses, but they have been unsuccessful. Now, I want you five," she pointed to DC Wright and four other officers, "To check on all carpet and upholstery cleaners in the area. As you know, the victims have all had an inexplicably high number of different fibres on their bodies. Far higher than normal, and fibres that don't equate to the ones in their immediate environments. We think our man might be in the carpet cleaning business."

She then turned to DC Stone.

"Let's see if we can get more details about people who own digital cameras. Find the major outlets in this area that stock them, and see if anyone remembers a recent purchase of one of the high end ones. The computer boys tell me that the image that came to me is quite high resolution – it'd have to be one of the top line Kodaks or better. I realise with everyone from Dixons to Jessops selling the damn things it's a slim chance, but we don't have that many avenues to pursue."

"Yes, certainly ma'am, I'll get on to that straight away."

The DC was pleased that she'd given him this line of enquiry to pursue as he himself was a bit of a computer buff.

"We shall have to get Morrison to take her photo, although I realise it won't be as good as one that was taken when she was alive. Then we can get it circulated in the hope someone recognises her. When you've got the photo I want it taken to every house, pub and shop in Brixham – someone must know this girl. Right that's all for now. Oh and by the way – I do appreciate how hard you've all been working on this case, and that some of you have had to cancel holidays. All I can say is when we catch this madman – and I stress the word *when* – you will all get the leave that's owing to you."

They all nodded by way of acknowledgement. Despite the fact Josephine had had lots of stick in the past from them, they knew she was fair and wouldn't ask them to do anything she wouldn't do herself.

* * *

Later that day Jessica phoned Josephine on her mobile.

"Hi Mum, how are you?"

"More to the point, are *you* okay?" Josephine asked.

"Don't worry, I know all about the message he left on your computer. So he's seen me, but I'm miles away and I feel safe. You're closer to him – you're the one in danger."

"I've got plenty of protection," she assured her.

"What, with one PC? If he's the sadistic maniac you all think he is, I doubt that will stop him."

Josephine shivered.

"Have you just called to frighten me Jessica, because if you have…"

"No, actually I phoned to tell you I'm coming back at the weekend."

"I'd rather you didn't Jessica, I'd feel better if you stayed in Nottingham."

"I'm not coming home. Dad phoned the other night, and he wants me to stay with him and

Marion."

"Oh I see," she said angrily.

"Look Mum, I have to meet her sometime, and Dad is upset because someone has slashed the tyres on her car."

"It's probably some other woman whose husband she's had an affair with," Josephine said haughtily.

"Mum, you sound like a bitter old spinster," Jessica said.

"I feel like one," she replied.

"How can you, when you've got that nice man," Jessica joked. "Anyway I must go now, I'll ring you from Dad's house," she said, before she put down the receiver.

Chapter 21

JOSEPHINE PUT ON HER CAP and gown before entering the forensic pathology department.

Brian Morrison came over and asked, "How are you?"

"It's not one of my best days, to say the least. Anyway, never mind about me, how's your wife and daughter?"

"They're fine, but I don't spend as much time with them as I'd like to, with the hours I work here. Jodie's starting nursery school soon," Morrison told her.

"It doesn't seem five minutes since she was a baby," Josephine reflected.

"I know, it's gone so fast," he agreed.

"I know it's difficult Brian, but you must spend more time with your family. Don't make the same mistake that I did – I hardly ever saw Tom and Jessica, and if I had my time over again I'd do things differently. Anyway, back to business. Can we go over your report on the body? I'm afraid we don't have an ID for the poor girl yet. I need a photograph of her face so the officers can circulate it for identification purposes."

"I've taken one already, but it does show the cuts on her neck."

"We can't show that to the public. I'll need another shot taken."

"That's not a problem, I'll get it done for you after you've viewed the body."

They walked over to the table and he drew back the green sheet.

"Such a pretty girl. What a waste," Josephine said emotionally.

"As you can see, her throat was cut from ear to ear. I agree with the police surgeon – she couldn't have cried out, as her windpipe was severed. The blood on the lamp post matches her blood group, I think she put her hand to her throat as her life's blood was ebbing away and then reached out to the post. She'd have lost consciousness very quickly and I don't think she suffered much, as there are no more injuries to her body. She had sex shortly before she died, but the interesting thing is when we tested the semen from her body in the lab, there were two different types. The only explanation for this is that she had sexual intercourse with two different men," Morrison said laconically.

Josephine thought for a moment or so.

"I wonder if perhaps she had sex with, say, her boyfriend, and then left him, and then the Ripper raped her before he murdered her?" she suggested.

"If that was the case, surely her boyfriend would see her home and not let her walk by herself at that time in the morning?" Morrison replied.

"That's if it *was* her boyfriend. I suppose it could have been a casual date, or someone she had met that evening. In fact, I could be on the wrong track here, but do you think she could have been a prostitute?" she suggested.

"It's a possibility she may have been. There was no bruising or damage to her vagina so I don't think force was used. She could just have had sex with two different men before she met her killer, and he may not have sexually assaulted her at all."

"Well, the original Jack The Ripper only murdered prostitutes. Our copycat killer's first two victims weren't in that trade. If this latest was a prostitute, or just had several sexual partners, the fact that she was slaughtered in the street, even though the date is different, leads me to think he is getting more like his mentor."

"I know young girls are quite scantily clad nowadays, but she was wearing a short black mini skirt and a low cut top that exposed her bra. It was difficult to see her clothing when we arrived at the scene because it was covered in so much blood, but she was provocatively dressed. In the killer's eyes she may have appeared to be a 'loose' woman. I've tested her for HIV, but I don't have the results yet. Apart from that she was quite a healthy young woman. See these marks on her neck?" He pointed to several blue and yellow bruises on the side of her neck. "I thought at first they were inflicted by the murderer but on closer examination, they appear to be quite old. I'd say they were lovebites."

"There's little doubt, if she wasn't a prostitute, she had an extremely active sex life. Even so, she didn't deserve to die like this," Josephine said.

"I've taped her body, and sent the tapes down to the lab. We can go there now and see if they have anything for us," Morrison suggested.

* * *

When they entered the Forensic Laboratory Gary Madison was sitting nearby looking in to a microscope. He looked up as he saw them.

"Hello there," he said to Josephine, "So we meet again."

"Have you got anything for me?" she asked.

"The fibres we detected are similar to those

found on the first two victims, but we didn't find so many. However, their content does suggest they came from carpets."

Josephine told them about her theory that the killer could be a carpet cleaner and asked for their opinion.

"I'd say that was quite possible. He'd be picking up different fibres each day which explains why we found so many. Despite the fact the last victim was outside and some may have blown away, there are still traces of them. If you went into someone's house and sat down on, say, a red carpet, the fibres would attach themselves to your clothes, but during the day the majority of them would come off, only leaving a few on your clothes. A carpet cleaner would visit many dwellings in a week and each would have a different carpet – nylon, wool, acrylic – and each would be a different colour. This would explain why all the fibres on these victims are similar in type and content, but not an exact match. We know that one man committed all the murders, and he and the fibres are the common thread. I'd say that there's a good chance he works in a profession similar to the one you describe," Madison said.

* * *

Jessica had reservations about meeting Marion, the new woman in her father's life, although she'd never have admitted this to her mother. She felt she needed to be friendly to Marion for her father's sake, and yet at the same time she couldn't help feeling distant towards her. They were living in Marion's home, a small cottage in Dartmouth. When Tom introduced Jessica to her, she was taken aback by Marion's resemblance to her mother, Josephine.

They had a meal at the cottage and then Tom proposed that they go for a drink at the local pub, The White Horse. It was only a mile or so away. Tom suggested they walked down the country lane to the pub. Jessica hadn't had the opportunity to speak to her father in private, but fortunately for her they had been in the pub for about ten minutes, when Marion noticed a woman she used to work with.

"Oh, I hope you'll excuse me for a moment Jessica, only I must have a quick chat with Christine, I haven't seen her in ages," Marion said as she stood up.

"That's fine, take your time," Jessica replied, pleased that she had got her father to herself for a while.

"Well, what do you think of her?" he asked.

"I hate to say this Dad, but she reminds me of

Mum."

"She's a good woman you know, Jessica."

"I'm sure she is, and if you're happy Dad, that's all that matters."

He was pensive for a moment or two before speaking.

"I still care for your Mum, it's just that we'd grown apart and become so indifferent to one another. It's a pity we couldn't work things out. How is she?" he asked her.

"Quite frankly, I'm worried about her. I suppose you know about this copycat killer as it's front page news, and now he's emailing messages to her."

"That's a worry. Has she got protection?" Tom asked.

"There's a PC guarding the house, and she's had a panic button installed, but I'm still worried about her."

"Do you think I should ring her?" Tom asked.

"I wouldn't Dad, she's got enough on her plate at the moment."

"But she must be so lonely," he added.

"Well, actually, she's seeing someone at the moment."

Tom looked shocked.

"Is she? Who's that then?"

"His name's Andrew. I think he's a psychiatrist, or something like that."

"It's Andrew Blythe, he's always fancied your Mum, and now she's free he's jumped in with both feet," he said angrily.

"Dad! Stop it, you sound jealous. You've got someone, why shouldn't Mum have a life?"

"You're right, I'm being selfish. It's just..." he turned his face away from Jessica "... I still love her," he whispered.

Just at that moment Marion came back and they quickly changed the subject.

* * *

It was a fine night as they walked down the lane back to the cottage.

"I take it you're staying the night?" Tom asked.

"Yes, I'll catch the train back tomorrow," Jessica replied.

"I'll drop you at the station before I go into work," Tom said.

"Okay, thanks Dad."

As they continued to walk along Jessica said,

"It was a nice meal Marion, thanks for inviting me."

"It was a pleasure, you're welcome anytime Jessica."

'She's not Mum but she's not a bad sort,' Jessica thought to herself. Just at that moment, a motorbike came speeding around the bend.

"Look out!" Tom shouted.

Jessica managed to jump out of the way just in time, but the bike hit Marion. Her body was thrown up into the air and landed in the hedge.

"Oh my God!" Tom screamed.

He quickly went over to where Marion lay, although he could hardly see her as it was so dark. Jessica followed him and began examining Marion.

"Oh God, is she dead?" he shouted at Jessica.

She felt Marion's wrist.

"I can feel a pulse," she told him.

Suddenly Marion groaned.

"Can you hear me?" Tom asked anxiously.

"It's just my leg, I can't move it, the pain's terrible" she said weakly.

"Where are the keys to the cottage, Dad?" asked Jessica

Tom fumbled in his pocket and gave her the key.

"I'll run on and phone for help, I'll be a lot quicker than you, stay here and look after Marion. Don't worry, I'm sure she'll be alright."

Luckily Jessica was wearing trainers with her jeans and she sprinted back to the cottage; it only took her five minutes. She phoned for the ambulance and told them how far down the lane from The White Horse the accident had happened. Then she ran into the kitchen and found a torch before going upstairs to get a blanket from the bed. Within minutes she was back with Tom and Marion.

"I've phoned for the ambulance, they shouldn't be long. How is she?" she asked as she covered Marion with a blanket.

"She's still conscious," Tom replied shakily. "Jesus! What a bloody maniac!"

"I've brought this, so the ambulance will be able to see us," Jessica said as she switched on the torch.

Ten minutes later the ambulance arrived, and after the paramedics had made Marion as comfortable as they could at the scene of the accident, they lifted her gently into the ambulance and drove to the nearest hospital.

After Jessica and Tom had waited anxiously for an hour or so in the corridor outside the accident and emergency department, a doctor came out to speak to them.

"She's a very lucky woman, your wife."

"She's not my wife – we live together."

"She has a broken leg and two cracked ribs; fortunately there doesn't seem to be any injury to the head or any concussion. but we'll keep her in a few days for observation," the doctor told him.

"Can I see her?" Tom asked.

"Yes, but just for a few minutes."

He went in alone and Jessica went to get a can of cola from the machine. Ten minutes later he came out of the room and walked down the corridor to where Jessica was sitting. She could see by the expression on his face, he was relieved.

"She's okay, and asked me to thank you for what you've done."

"I only went to get help – anyone would have done the same," Jessica replied.

"You know, you've got a lot of your Mum's qualities. You stayed cool in an emergency. I would never have thought of getting a torch and blanket. I was so panicky, I don't know how I'd have coped if you hadn't been there."

She slipped her arm through his

"Well, it's a good job I was then, wasn't it Dad'?" she said, smiling.

"Let's get a taxi back home. I don't know about you, but I could do with a stiff drink."

"We can't go yet," Jessica replied. "I've had to call the police – it was a hit and run."

"We can't tell them anything about the bike. I didn't even see the number, it was so dark, did you?"

"No I didn't. But it needs to be reported. He may have a dent on his bike caused by the impact."

Tom went quiet for a few moments.

"You know, it doesn't bear thinking about, she

could have been killed."

"So could we. Have you thought of that? He drove at us like a maniac. He could have killed any one of us."

"But surely it was an accident? Maybe he lost control of his bike?" Tom suggested.

"He was on the other side of the lane, with his headlight on, and he drove straight at us. This was no accident, Dad."

"I've come to the conclusion you're as suspicious and distrusting as your Mother," Tom told her.

Shortly afterwards two PCs arrived at the hospital and took a statement from Tom and Jessica about the accident. On the doctor's instructions they arranged to speak to Marion the following day, when her condition would have improved.

* * *

The next morning, Tom drove Jessica to the station and saw her safely onto the train. When she arrived back at her flat in Nottingham, she rang Josephine to tell her about the accident.

"Are you sure you're okay?" Josephine asked.

"I'm fine Mum, and so's Dad. Luckily Marion's injuries aren't too serious, but the point I'm making is, he drove straight at us."

Josephine knew her daughter well enough to realise she wasn't the sort to be unduly alarmed, in fact she'd usually make light of a serious situation.

"Do you think the man on the bike could be the killer, and he *meant* to hit you?"

"No, not really Mum. Oh, I don't know! I mean he had plenty of opportunity to get me when I was alone, if he'd wanted to. Why wait until I'm with Dad and Marion? It doesn't make sense. Maybe it was just an accident or some mad driver who was high on drugs," Jessica suggested.

"Listen, I want you to promise me you'll stay in Nottingham until this case is finished," Josephine told her.

"I will Mum. I've got an exam coming up soon, and I really need to study. So I probably wouldn't have been coming home until Christmas anyway."

"I'll find out what station the policemen who took your statement came from, and I'll get the accident report. Then the area can be searched for evidence. It's always possible something may have fallen off his bike on impact."

"Dad can tell you the spot if you ring him."

"I'll do that. Thanks for ringing, I love you."

"Me too. Oh, and Mum, *please* be careful"

"Don't worry, I'll be fine." Josephine said, but she didn't think for one moment she would be.

She put the phone down and then suddenly decided to ring Andrew. She looked at her watch, it was two thirty. *'He should be in his office,'* she thought as she dialled the number. His secretary answered.

"Hello, It's Detective Inspector Blake, is Doctor Blythe there?"

"I'm not sure. I'll have to check, if you could hold for a moment."

Music started to play on the line and as Josephine listened she thought *'How can she not be sure she sits outside his office! He's either there or he's not!'* A minute or so later she was just about to hang up, when he came on the line.

"I thought you'd left the country," she said sarcastically.

"I had a difficult case to attend to at Totnes Hospital – the patient had attempted to kill herself and was in a bad way. How was Bill's party?" he asked.

"Okay – I thought you could have at least phoned! I was expecting you to come, even if it was later."

He sounded vague and aloof.

"I couldn't – the case was complicated."

"It must have been, if you couldn't spare a minute to pick up your mobile," she replied.

He ignored Josephine's last remark.

"So he's struck again, but earlier this time?"

She was annoyed he had changed the subject but tried not to show it. "Yes we weren't expecting him to strike till the thirtieth. This victim was killed on a street in Brixham. So it resembled the Ripper's crimes more than the first two."

"He's becoming more daring with each murder. He took a real chance this time – he could easily have been seen," Andrew remarked.

"We've come to that conclusion. Although it was early morning when he struck, so there wasn't anyone about," Josephine replied.

Neither of them spoke for a few moments, and Josephine was waiting for him to suggest that they meet, but his final words were,

"I'll let you get on – I know you must be busy with this latest murder. If you need to discuss the case further, ring me and we can arrange a meeting with David Burke."

Josephine felt hurt, it was obvious to her he no longer wanted to see her, and she regretted becoming so emotionally involved. She felt in peril from the killer, and had thought Andrew would be there for her when she needed him. It was now apparent she was wrong.

"I'll let you know," she replied and hung up.

Her eyes filled with tears and she bit her lip as she tried to hold them back. Just then DC Sally James knocked on her door.

"Come in," she said.

"Are you okay ma'am?" Sally asked, noticing her glassy eyes.

"Yes, I'm fine, a bit of conjunctivitis I think," she lied. "I want you to check on an accident in which my daughter was involved."

"Is she alright?" Sally asked, slightly alarmed.

"Yes, she's fine. I just want details from whoever took the report at Totnes Hospital."

Josephine explained that the injured party was the woman who was living with Tom, and gave her all the relevant information. When she had written everything down Sally said

"I'll get on to that straight away, ma'am."

Josephine wondered if Tom or Jessica had seen Andrew at Totnes Hospital. Still, he'd have been in the psychiatric department, and they were in the Accident and Emergency. Jessica would have told her if she'd seen him.

"Sally, I'd like you to go the hospital and get a statement from Marion Walters. I'd go myself but you know how it is..."

"I understand that it would be awkward, ma'am. I'll take the statement, but are you sure you can spare me, as we're short staffed on this case?"

"I think it could be the killer who hit Marion, and that Jessica was the intended victim. I know I could be on the wrong track, but he does know

I have a daughter, as he's mentioned her in his email messages"

"I'll see what I can find out, ma'am," Sally replied.

Just as she was about to leave, Josephine said,

"While you're there I want you to see if you can find out if Doctor Blythe has been treating a patient on the psychiatric ward."

She knew in her own mind that what she had asked her DC to do was unethical, but felt she needed to know.

Chapter 22

JOSEPHINE WAS IN the incident room with the murder squad team. Two DCs had been making inquiries around the Brixham area, paying particular attention to the shops and pubs, showing the victim's photo in the hope that someone would recognise her. The first DC addressed Josephine and the team.

"It seems, ma'am, we have an ID for the victim. I showed her photo to Mr McGregor who's the manager of the Anchor pub in Brixham. He identified the photo as that of Melissa Jenkins, and by all accounts she drank in the pub most evenings. He went on to say that she'd often leave with a different man and although he didn't actually refer to her as a prostitute, he said he thought she was paid for her sexual favours, as she was never short of money."

"That seems to tie up with Brian Morrison's

report that there were two different types of semen found in her body. It's a possibility the killer had sex with her before he slit her throat, but I think the semen found was from two different customers, so to speak."

"The chances of them coming forward are remote," Bill remarked. "Especially if they're married."

Josephine turned to Bill

"I want you to go to the Anchor pub with DC Burton here, and put a bit of pressure on the owner. He must know who her regulars were."

"I'll go down there after two o'clock – he'll probably be busy with the lunchtime trade until then," Bill replied.

"How's the report on the carpet cleaning firms coming along?" Josephine asked

"We've contacted about a dozen so far, and we're going through a list of statements as to where the owners or employees of the firms were on the dates of the murders, and we are also checking their appointment books to see if Jane Fielding or Sheila Jones were ever customers," Bill told her.

"Right, Barnes," Josephine said as she turned to the DC, "I want you to go and speak to Martin Jones. Find out if his wife has had any carpets cleaned in the last few months."

"Okay ma'am. I'll get on to that right away."

"After you've spoken to Mr McGregor at the pub, you'll have to arrange to take him to the morgue to identity the body," she instructed Bill. "Right that's all for now, I want you all to keep me up to date on any developments or information you get," Josephine told everyone. They all dispersed as the briefing came to an end.

* * *

Josephine checked in on her computer to see it there was any email. The killer had sent another message.

Number three and you are no closer to catching me My murders will never cease but after five you can rest in peace.
Jack

Josephine's heart did not race with fear as it had done in the past. This time she felt an intense hatred for him.

"Yes, you have fooled me again, you bastard" she said loudly, "But I'll get you, if it's the last thing I ever do on this earth!"

A short while after she had received the message Josephine rang Roger Graham, the expert on Jack The Ripper and gave him details of the recent murder and the last two messages she had received from the killer.

"He knew you'd expect him to strike on the thirtieth of September. and probably thought you might put extra police on the streets. Although even if you had done that in Torquay, it would have been useless, as his next victim was found in a different area. In my opinion he's not an exact copycat of Jack The Ripper, which is obvious since this last date is different. I don't think he is completely obsessed with the Ripper. Having said that, if this last victim *was* a prostitute, the fact he slashed her on the streets and cut her throat was almost identical to the Ripper's third murder. I think he wants to impress you in a sick, demented, sort of way. Also, to outwit the police, he wants and needs to be as clever and elusive as the Ripper was," Graham said.

"We've got more technology and forensic science than they had in the last century, and he's forgetting that fact. We've discovered two types of semen in the victim's body, but we don't know if one belongs to the killer," Josephine added.

"There was never any evidence that Jack The Ripper raped his victims, and I don't think these are sexual murders, despite the fact he had sex with Jane Fielding," he commented.

"The forensic lab is doing tests on the semen found on the first victim, which we're almost certain belongs to the killer. If we get a match with the type of semen found on this latest victim it will determine whether he had sex with her before he slashed her throat. Although personally I agree with you – I don't think he had any sexual contact with her."

"I think he'll stop after he's murdered five," Graham announced.

"If you're right that means there's just two to go. And yet, I think that he gets so much satisfaction from killing, he'll go on taking lives until we catch him."

"I'm not a psychologist," he stated. "But as far as we know the Ripper only killed five."

"We haven't been able to stop his trail of destruction. If he kills again before we can catch him, I shall have no alternative but to leave the force," Josephine said, as she put down the phone.

* * *

An hour or so later her mobile rang she picked up the phone and pulled her aerial out to hear a rather strange eerie voice.

"Josephine?"

"Yes," she replied.

"I tried to get rid of your rival."

"What..? What are you talking about? Who is this?"

"You know who it is."

Her heart started to pound with fear and excitement. It was the killer! She quickly thought how she could get the call traced. As she spoke to him, she opened her office door and walked rapidly to the reception desk.

"That woman your husband left you for – I thought I'd get her out of the way."

She suddenly realised that *he* was driving the motorbike that ploughed into Marion as she walked along the country lane with Tom and Jessica. As she reached the front desk she quickly grabbed a pen and wrote on the blotter in front of the sergeant, IT'S THE KILLER! TRACE THIS.

"You could have killed my daughter," she told him.

"I know, but I didn't know she'd be with them," the killer said.

Despite the fact Josephine had no feelings for her ex-husband's lover, she didn't want her harmed in any way.

"Tom means nothing to me. She's done me a favour taking him off my hands," said Josephine.

"Okay, in that case I won't finish the job when she gets out of hospital."

Her heart was pounding so much at this point, she thought she was going to have another panic attack.

She felt like saying "I wish I could kill you. You murdering sick bastard!" But it took all her self-control and courage to say

"I'd like us to meet."

"We will, very soon. On my terms." The phone went dead.

A DC said to her "We've traced the call to a public phone box by the harbour. A squad car is on it's way there now, although I doubt we'll catch him, with all the crowds in town."

"Speak to the people in the area, and also see if anyone who was waiting to use the phone remembers him," Josephine said.

After she'd finished instructing the DC she went straight to the Chief's office to tell him what had happened. The Chief telephoned David Burke and Andrew Blythe to inform them of the telephone conversation, in the hope that they may be able to analyse what the killer said. He also hoped that they might be able to second guess his next move. After the Chief had spoken to Andrew he passed the phone over to Josephine. She didn't feel like speaking to Andrew again, but knew she'd have to if only in a professional capacity. She gave him all the details of the conversation.

"If he's made an attempt on Tom's girlfriend's life, I believe he's far more obsessed with you than we originally thought, and that you're in grave danger, Josephine," he told her. She wasn't as upset and frightened by this remark as she should have been.

"Well that's my problem, not yours," she said abruptly.

"Of course it's my problem, I do care about you Jo, you know I do."

"The only thing I know at the moment is that we've got to catch this madman, and quick."

* * *

She phoned Tom to tell him about her conversation with the killer and said she'd arrange for Marion to have police protection while she was in hospital.

He was understandably very angry and upset.

"Even though I've divorced you, your job is still destroying my life. Well I'll tell you this – if anything happens to Marion I shall hold you personally responsible."

"I've told the killer that you and Marion mean nothing to me. I don't think he'll try to harm her again."

"Oh, you don't, well I don't find that remark reassuring at all, you're no closer to catching him."

"Look, Tom, I can't tell you how bad I feel about what's happened, but my life's in danger as well."

"That's one of the disadvantages of your

profession. That's a risk *you* take, but when it starts to affect me and Marion, that's different."

She was hurt by his last remark. Obviously he was frightened but he didn't seem even slightly concerned that her life was in jeopardy, even though they'd spent the last twenty years together.

"I give you my word Tom, that you and Marion will have protection till he is caught."

"Don't bother, as soon as she's well enough to travel I'm taking her abroad. The chap I work with has a villa in Spain that's vacant at the moment," he told Josephine.

"I'll arrange for protection until you go. In fact, right up till you board the plane."

His voice was a little less fraught.

"Okay, I'll go to the hospital now and explain to Marion what's going on. I'll ring you later," he said and hung up.

When DC Sally James came into the office, Josephine bought her up to date with developments.

"There's a PC at the hospital now, and she'll be under guard twenty-four hours a day, until she leaves. I doubt he'll attempt to harm her again, now that he knows I don't want Tom back."

"Do you think your daughter's safe, ma'am?"

"I've telephoned her at University and told her to stay there, although I don't think he'll harm her."

"Oh, by the way ma'am, I've got the details on Doctor Blythe's patient. She's a schizophrenic, who's attempted suicide before several times, and she's on Ward eight."

"Right, thanks Sally"

"The odd thing is though, ma'am, her consultant at the moment is a Doctor Lloyd, it seems she hasn't seen Doctor Blythe for at least a month.

* * *

Josephine arrived home at about seven o'clock in the evening. The PC was sitting outside in a squad car. She nodded to him as she walked past, and wondered if she should ask him in for some refreshment, but she needed to be alone. So she made two rounds of sandwiches and a flask of coffee, and took them to the car.

"Thank you ma'am," the PC said, "This is much appreciated."

"I'd ask you in, but I'm having an early night," she told him

"Sleep well then, ma'am, and don't worry, I'll be here – should you need me, just press the panic button"

She returned to the house and started to pick at the sandwich she'd prepared for herself, but she had no appetite. She poured herself a glass of wine and sat on the balcony and looked out to sea. Her mind was disturbed and she felt agitated. Why did Andrew lie about seeing a patient? He could have made some other excuse for not turning up at Bill's party. It probably never occurred to him that she'd check up on him. Did he really care?. The night that they had made love had been wonderful, but maybe it was just pure lust to him, and not the emotional experience she had found it. She suddenly felt cold and frightened. No surely not, it was inconceivable. She looked at the sun setting behind the hills. It was surely impossible? She'd made love to this man. He was tender and caring wasn't he? It was ridiculous and yet…

She tried to take control of her feelings and get things into perspective.

'You're not thinking straight my girl! Is it any wonder after the things that have happened over the last few weeks? It's enough to make the most rational and level headed person somewhat demented and anxious. A cup of tea, that's what I need.'

She went into the kitchen, and as she plugged in the kettle the phone rang.

"Hello, it's Bill here."

Before he had time to finish his sentence, Josephine started to cry.

"Oh Bill, please come round, I think I'm going mad."

* * *

Twenty minutes later Bill's car pulled up outside Josephine's house.

"Anything wrong, sir?" the PC asked getting out of his car.

"No Constable, I've just come to go over some details with the Inspector," Bill said to him. He walked up to Josephine's door and rang the bell.

"I feel awful dragging you over here. I'm sure you've got better things to do," she said, as Bill took off his coat.

"I haven't actually. Joyce isn't speaking to me, and none of the lads were going to the club," he admitted. "Anyway even if I had something better to do, I'd still have come over."

Josephine started to cry and Bill put his arm around her.

"Now come on, it's not like you to get in a state."

"I just can't cope anymore, Bill."

"I'm not surprised, with what you've had to contend with this maniac. Now if you don't stop crying I shall leave. Have you eaten?" he asked.

"I'm not hungry."

"We'll see." He went into the kitchen, opened the fridge and took out a box of eggs. He opened the cupboard and started to hunt around amongst the bottles and tins.

"Here we are," he said as he held up a jar of dried herbs. Josephine could see there was no point in objecting so she sat back and left him to it. Some time later he placed two omelettes on the table and uncorked a bottle of white wine.

"Just eat, whether you're hungry or not," he ordered Josephine. Some minutes later she'd cleared her plate.

"That was delicious Bill, I never knew you could cook."

"I couldn't when I was married to Mary. I've had to teach myself since I've been living alone. I'd never admit this to the lads at the station, but I really enjoy it."

After she'd finished her second glass of wine Josephine began to unwind.

"Right. Out with it – what's wrong?" Bill asked.

She decided to tell him of the doubts she had about Andrew. She wouldn't have confided in Bill some years earlier, as there had been a lot of friction between them in the early days. In the past he'd have relished the fact she couldn't cope, as he was then rather against women in the force, but he'd come to like and admire her during the time they'd worked together. He knew she wouldn't have asked him to come if she hadn't been genuinely distressed.

When she had finished telling Bill that Andrew had lied about his whereabouts he said "Surely you don't think he's involved in these murders?"

"Well, no, of course not... oh I don't know anything anymore Bill. I can't think straight."

"If you ask me he's probably seeing another woman, and that's why he's lying."

"Oh Bill," Josephine laughed even though she was upset, "Trust you to think of that."

"I'm only being logical. So you slept with the guy – that doesn't mean he has to be faithful."

"How did you know that?" Josephine asked amazed.

"I could tell you fancied him by the way you acted."

"I didn't realise you were so observant."

"I'm a copper aren't I?" Bill said.

"Yes, but normally men are too insensitive to pick up on things like that. I know I sound emotional, but I really thought he cared," Josephine confessed.

"Maybe he does, but doesn't want commitment."

"Neither do I," she told Bill.

"Well look at it this way. If he hadn't got another woman, why lie?"

"I suppose you're right," Josephine said lethargically. "I just feel I'm losing my grip on things."

Bill took hold of her hand and spoke to her like a big brother.

"Let's put things into perspective Josephine. We're all after this copycat murderer. The crimes are particularly gruesome and horrific – even I've had nightmares, I don't mind admitting. But you're the one he's contacting by email. Then he even decides to get rid of Tom's bit of stuff, because he thinks she may have hurt you. So obviously the guy's obsessed. You finally find someone you care for, sleep with him and then find he's been deceiving you. It's enough to make the toughest person lose their marbles!"

Bill had a very forthright way of putting things.

"Now, you're a good looking woman for your age and you haven't got a bad figure. If you weren't like a sister to me, I'd fancy you myself. I suggest you give your doctor friend the elbow, and find yourself another man."

She gave Bill a hug.

"I knew I could depend on you to bring me back down to earth, you're just what I needed."

"Glad I could be of some help. Do you want me to stay?"

"No, I'll be fine Bill, I've got the PC outside."

"I'll be off then. Oh by the way, I almost forgot to tell you, I spoke to Martin Jones. He said they'd had no-one in to clean their carpets, but said that his late wife's friend had had her whole house cleaned He gave me the friends' name and address. It was a Mrs Jean Myers, so I went to see her. She said the day she had all her carpets cleaned, the man in question had asked her to go out, as he said it would be far easier for him to get on with his work if the house was empty. So she decided to go on a shopping trip for the day to Plymouth with Sheila Jones. When Sheila arrived Mrs Myers wasn't ready, so Sheila chatted to the cleaner while she was waiting for her. It may be a longshot, but if it's the man we're looking for she could have bumped into him again after the aerobics class. Since she'd met him beforehand, she'd have had no qualms about chatting to him – in fact she may even have accepted a lift home. I know it could be pure supposition, but it's something I feel needs looking into."

"Did you show Jean Myers the photofit picture of the man?" Josephine asked.

"Yes I did, even though it's not a very reliable picture. She said she wasn't certain it was the same man, but said the photo looked familiar."

"What's the name of the firm?" Josephine asked.

"The Devonshire Carpet Cleaners, their offices are based in Churston."

"We'll pay them a visit first thing tomorrow morning," Josephine stated.

"I don't suppose they'll be open until nine o'clock – do you want me to pick you up?" Bill asked.

"No it's okay, I'll meet you at the station. I can get the PC outside to take me in the morning. I'll see you at the station just after eight." Josephine walked him to the front door.

"He must be bored sitting out there all night," Josephine said to Bill as she looked at the PC in the police car.

"In my day he'd be standing outside the house all night. At least he's got the warmth and comfort of the car. I can remember guarding someone once – I never sat down for hours," Bill grumbled.

"Go home, before you start reminiscing about the 'good old days', or 'bad old days', whichever way you look at it," she said as she pushed him out of the door.

"Oh, by the way Bill."

"What?" he asked

"Thanks for coming."

Chapter 23

THEY WERE LATE leaving the station the next morning, as a girl had come forward, saying she was a friend of the murdered girl Melissa Jenkins. Apparently they had shared a bedsit together in the past. She told them that Melissa was at one time studying for a degree at Plymouth University. but had found it impossible to manage on the student grant, and had met a group of rather seedy characters who suggested she occasionally had sex with them for extra money to make ends meet. That's all it was to start with. Whether she became used to the extra money or was depressed by the fact that she had to resort to such measures just to enable her to eat and buy the books she needed for the course, Theresa Parker wasn't sure, but eventually Melissa left university and worked as a prostitute full time.

Josephine was saddened and depressed, that

such a good looking and talented girl should have had to resort to a life on the streets. She realised most students found it hard to manage, financially especially if they had to move away from home. Those who lived with their parents and went to local colleges and universities seemed to be at an advantage. Fortunately Theresa Parker had Melissa's home address in Sheffield. Melissa's mother was divorced and it seemed she wasn't on speaking terms with her daughter, as they hadn't contacted each other for two years. Theresa gave Josephine both the mother's address and her own, and she asked if she could be notified of the date of the funeral. When she had left the station Bill said

"Shall we ring the mother?"

"I think it would be better if we contacted her local police in Sheffield, and ask them to go to see her personally," replied Josephine. "Even though she hasn't had any contact with her daughter, she probably still loved her. You never lose that bond with a child, no matter what conflicts or barriers come between you. I think she'll be dreadfully upset that she's been alienated from her daughter in the last two years, and the fact that she died in such horrific circumstances will make it much worse to bear."

"I suppose she'll want to travel down to Devon when she hears the news, so I'll pass all the details on to their police department, so she can contact us to make arrangements," Bill said.

"That's fine Bill. Will you do one more thing for me, before we visit the carpet cleaners?"

"I seem to be forever doing you favours lately," he smiled, "What is it?"

"Go and see if there are any messages from him on my email. I just couldn't face that computer today, in fact I dread using it. I think I'm becoming computer phobic, if there's such a thing!"

He left the office and returned ten minutes later.

"All quiet today, no messages from lover boy."

"Don't call him that, even in jest, the thought of that maniac repulses me."

"I'm sorry, I wasn't thinking," Bill replied.

* * *

The police car drew up outside Devonshire Carpet Cleaners, which was situated on the outskirts of Churston. It was quite a large building, which surprised Josephine, as she was expecting smaller premises. They showed their ID cards at reception, and were taken up to the manager's office on the second floor. They explained to Mr Gardner, the manager, what sort of information they needed.

"We cover most of the south Devon region," he began, "And sell franchises to people, and they trade under our name. They are set up with a van, and all the necessary equipment. Now, let's see, we have four agents in the Torbay area, two in Torquay, one in Paignton and another in Brixham."

"So if we give you the client's address, would you be able to tell us which of the four Torbay agents carried out the job?" Bill asked him.

"No, I'm afraid not, unless the customer in question had the receipt with the contractor's address on," he replied.

Josephine asked Bill if Jean Myers had shown him a receipt.

"Unfortunately she couldn't find it, but she did remember it had your name written across the top," Bill replied.

"Yes, she would, you see, all our receipts have Devonshire Carpet and Upholstery Cleaners printed across the top, and then individual contractors would put their own stamp at the bottom," Gardner explained.

"Let's just say someone bought a franchise. Would they work alone or employ staff?" asked Josephine.

"I've got a list of names here, let's see," he removed a file from the cabinet and placed it on his desk. After looking through it he continued.

"Here we are: all franchises were purchased singly, except the one in Torquay. Two partners went into business together. I'll get my secretary to photocopy these for you. Some of the owners may employ staff if they have a heavy work load, some may be registered, or they may just use casual labour for the day, if it's a big job. For example, if they're lucky enough to land the contract to clean the carpets in, say, a big hotel, they may need casual staff for a week or so.

"When people first buy our franchises, though, they tend to do all the work single-handed until they're established, because to start with they may not get enough work to justify employing someone."

"Yes, I can see that," said Josephine. "I suppose if they've used their savings or had a loan to start up, there probably isn't much cash left."

"Yes, we've had people who've used their redundancy money to start the business. Of course, in this area you've got all the hotels and guest houses, so there's probably more work than for firms in the city," added Gardner, pressing the intercom button on his desk.

"Jean, could you possibly come in for a moment?"

His secretary entered the office. Gardner handed her some papers from the file.

"Will you photocopy these for me?" Turning

to Josephine and Bill he asked, "How many copies do you need?"

"Just two copies of each firm in the area should be enough," replied Bill.

The secretary returned with the copies a few minutes later. Josephine stood up.

"Well, thank you for your co-operation, Mr Gardner," she said, as he gave her the paperwork.

"I wouldn't like to think that any of the people who have bought our franchises were involved in any way in these dreadful murders. The papers are full of them at the moment," he said in a serious voice.

"There may be no connection whatsoever, it's just that a friend of one of the victims had a carpet cleaned by one of your agents. And we have to look into every piece of information that we receive," Josephine responded.

"Yes, I can appreciate that," he said, as he shook their hands. "Please don't hesitate to contact me, should you need any more information."

Josephine and Bill thanked him again for his time, and left.

* * *

On the way back to the station, Bill made a suggestion.

"We've got telephone numbers for all these addresses. Couldn't we ring them to see who had the job of cleaning Jean Myers' carpets?"

"That would save time," agreed Josephine, "But I want you to visit all the others, as there's always the possibility that the firm who cleaned her carpets have no connection with our enquiries, even though the man knew Sheila Jones slightly."

After an hour or so of phone calls, they discovered that Roger Cleves, who had the Paignton branch of Devonshire Carpet Cleaners, had done the job in question. They hadn't spoken to him personally, but his secretary had gone through the appointment book and found Jean Myers' name and address; she also told them that Cleves was doing a job at a guest house in Chelston, and would be back in the office around 5p.m., and then gave them his mobile phone number.

They made a note of the number, but decided not to contact him, just in case he was the man they were after. The last thing they wanted to do was to warn him that they were on his trail. Josephine instructed his secretary not to inform him of their telephone call, which alarmed the young woman slightly, but she agreed to the request.

"We'll send a car round to the address in Chelston, a plain clothes DC in his own car.

Cleves may get suspicious if he sees a police car. Tell them to follow him, just in case he doesn't go straight back to the office, and to contact us as soon as he leaves," she looked at her watch; it was two thirty.

"I think I've just got time for a quick snack," she said, and made her way to the station canteen.

* * *

Josephine was just finishing her cheese salad when Andrew Blythe walked into the canteen. She was quite taken aback, and nearly choked on her last piece of cheese. She reached for her glass of orange juice and took a large gulp. As he sat down opposite her, he said in a pleasant voice,

"Hello, how's it going?"

"Er... Fine... I'm surprised to see you here though, I thought you were tied up with that case at Totnes hospital," she replied with an edge in her voice.

"I was, but it's all sorted out now."

"What exactly was the problem?" she asked.

"It's rather unethical to discuss the health of my patients," he replied.

"I'm sure it is," snapped Josephine, "Especially when they don't exist!"

"What do you mean? Of course I have a patient there." Andrew looked surprised by Josephine's outburst.

"Perhaps you do, but you didn't visit them on the night of Bill's party. In fact, you haven't been near the hospital in over a month."

"How did you know?" he gasped in amazement.

"In case you haven't noticed, Andrew, I'm a police inspector. If you were seeing someone else, you could at least have had the decency to tell me to my face. Surely I deserve that?"

"I'm not seeing anyone... Well, I am, but it's not how you imagine," he said in defence.

"I don't 'imagine' it to be anything. All I know is that you've lied to me on several occasions, and to be perfectly candid, Andrew, I have enough stress at the moment. And if I ever do enter another relationship, it will have to be with someone I trust.

"It's bad enough with this maniac serial killer at large, having to wonder when he'll strike again, or send me one of his sick messages. I don't want the added pressure of wondering where you are, or why you lied to me. And if you're the brilliant psychologist you think you are, you'll be able to see that."

Josephine stood up quickly, knocking her chair over, and stormed out of the canteen, hurrying back to the quiet of her office.

Andrew followed her close behind her.

"What do you want?" Josephine asked in exasperation, "I've said all I've got to say. I'm very busy. Now will you please leave?"

"Not until you've heard what I have to say," pleaded Andrew.

Josephine sighed.

"Okay, but you'd better make it quick."

"You were right, I wasn't at the hospital," he admitted. "I didn't like lying to you, but I didn't seem to have a choice. Frances, my ex-wife phoned me."

"And you went running!" exclaimed Josephine.

"It wasn't like that," continued Andrew, wearily, "She was concerned about our son, Luke. He lives in London, and he'd got in with the wrong crowd. They'd supplied him with heroin, and I'm afraid he'd developed a real habit. I travelled to London with Frances, in the hope of persuading him to go into a clinic for treatment. I had to stay up there until I was sure he would start on the medication. When you're detoxing, the first forty-eight hours are the worst.

"Frances has stayed in London with him, but I'm in constant touch by phone. I think he's got over the first hurdle, and I hope they'll be able to wean him off drugs permanently. The hardest part was getting him to admit he had a habit in the first place, that was a real problem. When he did come to terms with it, he said he really wanted to kick the habit, but it's so hard to do. I've seen so many people overdose on drugs, and I did think at one stage we might lose Luke too."

Andrew sat down heavily, and put his head in his hands.

"To think of all the people I've counselled in my career, all the problems I've helped people to solve, and I didn't even know what was happening to my own son. I should have been there for him sooner. What sort of father am I?" he uttered in despair. Josephine knelt down by the side of the chair, and took Andrew's hand in both of hers.

"It wasn't as if you were too late. He hasn't overdosed, and you've caught the problem in time. When your child is at the other side of the country, how can you know what's really going on in their lives? I suppose I'm fortunate that Jessica has never experimented with drugs. It could be because I've discussed some of my drug-related cases with her in the past, so she knows how drugs can destroy lives. I'm sure Luke will get through this, and he's got you and Frances to support him."

Andrew looked up at her with tears in his eyes.

"You've got so much on your own plate, and yet you've found the time to listen to my problems."

"Just call me Superwoman," she joked. "What

I don't understand is why you just didn't tell me all this at the time. Why all the secrecy?"

"I thought you would be angry because I'd stayed with Frances in London."

"Why should I?" she replied, "Unless you slept with her."

"No, we had separate rooms. We've been divorced for some time now; she did have another man, but it didn't work out."

"I'm surprised you two didn't get back together, both being unattached, so to speak."

"I stopped loving her a long time ago. We were never really compatible. But I couldn't let her cope with all this on her own, and obviously I needed to be there for Luke too."

"You thought I'd be jealous!" announced Josephine, suddenly realising what Andrew meant.

"Yes, I suppose I did," he admitted.

"So you think I'm that immature! I thought you had a higher opinion of me than that."

"If I thought you'd gone back to Tom, or any other man, I'd be insanely jealous," he admitted.

"I felt so close to you when we made love, and I'm really glad you're here now. I'm so afraid of this Ripper, and I think if we don't catch him soon I could end up being one of his victims. As you know, he's already tried to kill Tom's girlfriend. It's really unnerving how much he's obsessed with me."

Andrew stood up and put his arms around her.

"Don't worry, we'll fight this together. We won't let him win." He kissed her gently. "I love you, Jo."

Just at that moment Bill Hughes burst into the room. Andrew and Josephine moved apart.

"Roger Cleves is on the move, ma'am, he's just loading his machinery into the back of his van, outside the guest house in Chelston."

"Right Bill, let's keep in radio contact with that DC," said Josephine. Snatching up her bag and coat, she smiled at Andrew and set off for the car park.

* * *

Roger Cleves drove straight back to his office in Paignton, just as his secretary had said he would, and the journey passed without any unusual occurrences. He was an attractive man, in his late thirties, with dark hair, and as soon as she saw him, Josephine felt that it was just not possible that he could be responsible for sending her bizarre email messages, let alone slashing women to death.

Cleves was very surprised to see a police car waiting outside. Josephine and Bill followed him into the office, and showed him their ID cards.

Josephine noticed immediately that he had a new Pentium II computer on his desk.

"We've been given your address, and the addresses of the other agents in your area by Mr Gardner, at head office," she began.

"I haven't done anything wrong, have I?" interrupted Cleves, looking confused. He babbled on, "I mcan, although we sometimes use powerful chemicals, I always dilute them properly, and I always make sure I tell the customers to keep their windows open for at least two hours after I've finished. There was that one man who had an asthma attack, and we had to call an ambulance for him."

"It's nothing like that," interrupted Josephine. "Now if you'll just listen, Mr Cleves, I'll explain why we're here. I think you cleaned some carpets for Ms Jean Myers, who lives in Barton?"

"The name rings a bell, but I'd have to check my diary."

"Your secretary has already checked the appointment book for me, and the name and address were in there."

"I suppose I must have done then... Sometimes I'm so busy I forget the names." He leafed through the diary and appointment book, to check for himself.

"Yes, here it is. Come to think of it, I do remember the lady now. She had her whole house cleaned, but originally she only wanted the lounge, stairs and hall carpet doing. I offered to do the rest of the house for an extra twenty pounds, and she took me up on it. I seem to remember that she went out for the day, and I was able to get on in peace. Sometimes, customers like to stay and watch you steam cleaning, whether they think you're not going to do a good job, I don't know, and sometimes the children get under your feet..." He started to rattle on again, in a nervous way that made Josephine and Bill think that perhaps he did have something to hide. Josephine interrupted him.

"Can you remember whether there was another woman at the house when you arrived?"

"No, I don't think so... Oh, hang on, yes, they were going out together for the day. The other lady told me that her lounge suite badly needed cleaning, and I said I could always give her an estimate."

"That woman was brutally murdered four days later."

The colour drained from Cleves' face.

"Oh my God! Was she one of the copycat Ripper's victims?" he asked shakily.

"Yes, I'm afraid she was. Didn't you recognise her picture in the newspaper?" asked Bill.

"I can't say I did, to be honest." He looked over at them, as they stared back at him, and then he suddenly realised that he was a suspect.

"Surely you don't think that I...?" He started to tremble.

"We're not accusing you of anything, Mr Cleves," said Josephine soothingly, "We just want any information you can give us."

"I don't know what to say, I only spoke to her for a couple of minutes, and then they left."

"Do you work alone?" asked Bill.

"Most of the time. I only bought the franchise six months ago. I'd been unemployed for about a year, and then my mother died and left her house to be split four ways, between me and my brother and two sisters. We ended up with about fifteen thousand each, after the funeral had been paid for, and the solicitors' fees. I was going to use the money for home improvements, but I was so bored at home. Until I was made redundant, I'd never been out of work, in over twenty years. So I discussed it with my wife, and decided to invest in a franchise with Devonshire Carpet and Upholstery cleaners. My wife's got a little part-time job, and we've got two children." He continued to ramble on, as if he wanted to tell them his whole life story.

"As you know, there's not a lot of work in Devon, so I decided that my only hope was to start up in business for myself, and I'd got enough money to do so."

"Was it difficult to begin with?" enquired Bill.

"Yes, I was very worried I wouldn't be able to manage, as I'd never done anything like it before, but Devonshire Cleaners send you on a training course, and lease you a van for a year, and you get all the necessary equipment."

"How's the business doing?" ask Josephine.

"Well, it's ticking over, I'm making a living. There's not a lot of money to be made from domestic jobs, unless they have the whole house cleaned, but the guest houses and hotels are good jobs, when you can get them. I've just come from doing a guest house in Chelston," he told them, unaware that they had followed him from there.

"Do you ever employ casual staff?"

"No, I can't really afford to, but if I get a big job, my brother sometimes helps me out."

"Right. I think that's all for now. You will need to give us a blood sample, for DNA profiling purposes. You have the right to refuse to do this, but if you do so, it may go against you. We may also need to check your van for fibres," stated Josephine.

Roger Cleves looked scared to death.

"Look, I swear on my children's lives... I couldn't harm a fly!"

"Then once we've tested your blood sample, we can eliminate you from our enquiries."

"OK, I'll do it, I have nothing to hide," he said,

adamantly.

"Very well, if you could come to Torbay Police station tomorrow, the police doctor will take a sample," Bill instructed him.

"Any particular time?"

"Can you come in around nine o'clock?"

Cleves looked at his diary.

"Yes, that's fine, my first appointment isn't till eleven."

"We shall also have to send the forensic team out to remove sample fibres from your van, it shouldn't take more than a couple of hours, so it shouldn't disturb your schedule," added Josephine.

They left Roger Cleves in something approaching a state of shock, and made their way to the car.

"I don't know about you," said Bill as they drove toward the station, "But I could do with a drink." He looked at his watch. "What about it? We're off duty in half an hour."

For once Josephine agreed, so they changed course and headed for the Torbay Arms.

* * *

They sat in the quaint little pub near the harbour, mulling over the interview with Cleves.

"Do you know, Bill, at one point, I really

thought we were on to something," sighed Josephine, disappointedly.

"We may still be, we're watching the house, remember, and it may just be a case of waiting for the DNA results before we can make a move."

"I don't for one minute think the test will prove anything. I've just got a feeling... he's not the man we're after."

Bill took a long drink from his pint.

"I agree that on the surface he appears to be a normal, happily married family man, but then, look at Christie. Remember that friend of Blythe's, you know, the expert on serial killers..."

"David Burke," Josephine reminded him.

"That's him, well, even he said that these men appear to be normal pleasant people, like your friend, neighbour, or brother."

"I know what you mean, Bill, it's just that I really don't believe he's the Ripper."

"Your female intuition has never been wrong in the past, but there's always a first time!"

* * *

The following lunchtime Josephine had a call from Brian Morrison, who asked her to go over to his office. After a brief hello, Morrison explained the reason for his call.

"I've got the results back from the DNA test

on the semen found in Melissa Jenkins' body. There were two types, both have been tested, and neither matches up with that found on Jane Fielding's body. As we're more or less certain that the Fielding sample came from the killer, it's obvious that he didn't have sex with Melissa Jenkins before he murdered her."

"I didn't think he'd had sex with or raped Melissa. I suppose now it's been confirmed that she did work as a prostitute, we can assume the semen is from two of her customers. The chances of either of them coming forward are virtually nil, they're probably married men with families."

"I understand Mrs Jenkins is coming down to formally identify the body, although we already have a positive ID from her friend."

"That's right," said Josephine sadly, "she hasn't seen her for a couple of years, but I wouldn't imagine that would make the ordeal of seeing your daughter on a slab any less terrible."

"I'll make sure she's tidied up before her mother sees her," Morrison reassured her.

"Did I tell you we've got a suspect? Well, I can hardly call him that. Personally I don't think for one moment that he's involved, but he did clean carpets for Jean Myers, a friend of Sheila Jones, and he spoke to Sheila at the house. He's agreed to give a blood sample for DNA profiling, but I doubt we'll get a match. We've sent his overalls to the lab, and forensics are checking his car and van, for fibres, so I'd like you to liaise with them, and see if anything matches up with what we've got from the victims."

"I'll do all I can, you know that Jo."

"Thanks, Brian, but I feel that no matter what we do, it's hopeless. How are we ever going to catch him when he always seems to be one step ahead of us?"

* * *

Josephine had just walked into the station when Bill came rushing to meet her.

"There's another message on your email!"

Josephine hurried to her computer, and her heart sank when she read the screen.

Just to remind you Josephine. Only two to go and then you can rest in peace.
Jack

Josephine slumped in her chair.

"He's sent a similar message to this one before. You know what this means, Bill," she said, her heart pounding, "I'm going to be victim number five."

Chapter 24

Roger Cleves pushed away his half-eaten plate of steak and kidney pie and chips.

"Can't you shut those bloody kids up?" he shouted into the kitchen.

"You've only been in the house for half an hour and it's getting on your nerves already. You want to have them all day, like me, then you'd have something to moan about," said his wife, as she came into the dining room holding a tea towel. She looked down at his plate.

"It's not like you to leave your dinner, not when it's your favourite. I cooked it specially, although I wish I hadn't bothered now."

"I'm sorry, love, it's just that I've got a lot on my mind at the moment."

"That's understandable. It must have been awful, having to give that blood sample, but you're not involved, so what have you got to worry about?"

"Are you sure all the dates in the diary are correct?" he asked her.

"Yes, I'm sure. I think it's ridiculous that you should have to account for yourself on all the dates that the murders occurred," she commented.

"They haven't asked me yet, but I want to make sure I get my facts right when they do."

"But you're in every night, except when you have a big job on and have to work late."

"Look, the first murder was on August thirtieth, and we were out at Samantha and Joe's, it's here in the diary. The second was September eighth, but we didn't go out that night."

"I can tell them that we were both at home watching TV."

"But your evidence doesn't count for anything, because you're my wife!"

"For God's sake Roger, calm down! You're acting as though you're going to have to appear in court."

"What about the last date, September twenty-fifth? What were we doing then?"

Nothing, as far as I know. Hang on," she said, rechecking the diary, "My mum and dad came over for a meal, do you remember? And we played cards afterwards."

"What time did they leave?"

"I'm sure it wasn't till eleven."

"That's it! I remember now. Your dad had too much to drink, and I had to phone for a taxi for them." He jumped up and kissed his wife. "They'll vouch for me, I couldn't possibly have been in two places at the same time!"

"I really don't know why you were worrying in the first place."

"Well, you know what the police are like when they get hold of something. I mean, this Ripper chap has been headline news for weeks now. They must be under a lot of pressure to arrest someone for the murders, and they have been known to fabricate evidence."

"Do stop worrying now. Do you want me to warm your dinner up in the microwave?"

"No thanks love, give it to the dog. I wouldn't mind a can of lager though."

His wife took his plate into the kitchen, and came back with a cool can from the fridge and a glass. As Cleves poured his drink he continued his train of thought, "And that's another thing..."

"What is?" asked his wife, perplexed.

"Well, Phil's been helping me out on some of the big jobs, and I've been paying him cash in hand. What if the police find out about that?"

"They're not the Inland Revenue or Social Security, I'm sure they wouldn't be interested. I'm sure they're only interested in catching this killer, and to be honest, the quicker they do, the better, as far as I'm concerned. I'm afraid to go out at nights, I don't mind telling you."

* * *

"I've just had the report back from the Path lab. They couldn't find many fibres on Roger Cleves' overalls, although there were more in his van, and some of them do match up with those found on the victims," Josephine told Bill.

"That's the most conclusive piece of evidence we've got so far, surely he must be our man?" remarked Bill.

"I have to agree, and yet the baffling thing is, all the dates and times of his alibis check out. Unless there are a lot of people lying and covering up for him, it seems impossible that he could have been free at the times the murders were committed," replied Josephine.

"Since we're as certain as we can be that the semen on Jane Fielding's body is the murderer's, we need to get those DNA test results back as soon as possible. Without that, I don't think we've got enough to arrest him."

"You know, Bill, I still don't think he's the one responsible for these crimes."

* * *

Two days later, Roger Cleves was brought into the station for questioning. In the interview room, Josephine pressed the record button on the tape recorder, and stated the date, time and the names of the officers present, before beginning to talk to Cleves.

"Despite the fact that your alibis for the dates of the murders have been checked, and do appear to be reliable, and the results of your DNA profile test do not match with the sample found on the body of the first victim, we do have a match for the fibres found on the victims. We found these fibres on your overalls, and in your van. Can you give us any explanation as to why this should be the case?"

Cleves looked frightened and confused.

"I wasn't worried about giving you the blood sample, as I knew it wouldn't match with the semen found on that poor woman. My wife is the only person I've had sex with since we got married. My God, in twelve years I've never once been unfaithful, let alone had sex with a woman and then murdered her!" He put his head in his hands and groaned.

"I think I need a solicitor. I've done nothing wrong. This is a nightmare. I'm not the man you're after, I wouldn't hurt anybody, not even a fly." He looked across at Josephine.

"I can't even stand the sight of blood. One of the kids had a nosebleed the other day and it made me feel sick. According to the papers, this Ripper's been slashing their bodies, there's no way I could do that."

"If we could find a plausible explanation for why these fibres match, we could eliminate you from our enquiries, Mr Cleves," interjected Bill.

Josephine felt genuinely sorry for the man sitting opposite her. She was utterly convinced of his innocence. After the events of the previous few weeks, and all the email messages she had received, she felt certain that if she ever did come across the murderer she would know him at once.

"Please try and think, Roger. Have you lent your van to anyone?" she asked.

"No... I mean, I don't think so... I've racked my brain for some sort of solution – if I had one I'd tell you."

Josephine knew they were coming up against a brick wall, and that to continue to badger him would be pointless. She glanced at her watch.

"Interview suspended at eleven seventeen. Would you like some tea?"

"Yes please. Do you mind if I smoke?"

"No, you go ahead. We'll get the tea, won't we Sergeant?" she said, looking meaningfully at Bill. "I'll leave you with the PC."

"I know you prefer the gentle touch," said Bill on the way to the canteen, "But this is ridiculous. You're treating him far too softly."

"So how would you treat him? I mean, let's face it, not even you think he's guilty."

"I'll admit he doesn't seem the type, and there's no DNA match, but what about these bloody fibres? It's a complete mystery."

"There is an explanation, Bill, we just haven't found it yet."

* * *

Back in the interview room Roger Cleves lit a second cigarette. As he placed the lighter back on the table, he thought *'I must remember to give this back to Phil.'* Suddenly another thought occurred to him.

'No! Surely not! So he's helped me out, but he wouldn't... Would he? I never should have paid him cash in hand...' his mind was in turmoil.

'But he's a nice bloke... he couldn't possibly be involved in anything like this, could he? No, the idea's ridiculous.'

He wrestled with his conscience, trying to decide whether to say anything about Phil's involvement in the carpet cleaning business. Finally he came to a decision.

'I'd rather be in trouble with the tax people than be a suspect in a murder case.'

* * *

Josephine and Bill returned, and placed a paper cup of tea in front of him.

"Thanks," he said, stubbing out his cigarette. He cleared his throat.

"You know, it may be nothing, but..."

"Hang on," interrupted Josephine, pressing the record button, "Interview resumed at eleven thirty-two, those present are Doctor Roger Cleves, DI Blake, DS Hughes and PC Roberts. Carry on, Roger."

Cleves hesitated.

"It's probably nothing. I had an idea, but..." he trailed off.

"Look Mr Cleves, if there's anything at all you can tell us that would help us solve this case, it's your duty to do so. Your idea may or may not be relevant, but we won't know if you don't tell us. I don't want to keep you here any longer than is necessary. And what about your wife?" Josephine reminded him, "She must be sick with worry, and I'm sure you'd like to get home to her as soon as possible."

"Okay, okay, you've made your point. It's just that from time to time I call on a chap called Phil

Walker. We're not supposed to take on casual workers, as everyone's usually vetted by Devonshire Cleaners, and anyone operating their equipment is supposed to be trained and properly insured. But I can't afford to employ someone officially, even on a part time basis, so when I get a big job, or I've more work than I can manage single-handed, I get him along and pay him in cash. It suits us both, no questions asked."

"And do you think this Phil Walker could be involved in these murders?"

"Good Lord no! Phil's no murderer. He's a great bloke. It's just that..." he stopped half way through a sentence. Bill urged him to finish what he was saying.

"Do carry on, sir, we won't be reporting this to the Inland Revenue, if that's what you're worried about."

"He's worked with me on a few jobs in the last few weeks," Cleves continued.

"He didn't work with you on the Jane Myers job, did he? You said previously that you were alone on that one," said Josephine.

"I did do the job by myself, but I've just remembered that he called at the house, just as I was finishing. He'd got the address from my secretary, because he wanted to see me to find out if I had any more work for him."

"And had Jean Myers and Sheila Jones returned

from their day out at this point?"

"They arrived a few minutes later."

"Did Walker speak to them at all?"

"Yes, he did. In fact, he was laughing and joking with them. I remember thinking at the time 'come on Phil, you could be helping me put all this gear away in the van, instead of chatting up the women.'"

"So how often does he work for you?" asked Bill.

"About once or twice a week, usually."

"Do you provide him with overalls?"

"Yes, of course. You have to wear them, the chemicals would ruin ordinary clothes."

"And do you pick him up in your van, when you're going to a job?" queried Josephine.

"Sometimes. Other times he might make his own way to the job, by car."

"Does he give you the overalls back, when you've finished for the day?"

"No, he usually goes home in them. My wife would be happy to wash them in with mine, but he's never asked."

"Right, thank you, you've been very helpful," said Josephine, winding up the interview. "One last thing, do you have Phil Walker's address?"

"It's somewhere in Churston, leading down the lane to Dartmouth. I'm afraid I can't remember it off the top of my head. It's in my diary at home though, you can phone my wife and she could get it for you."

"Interview terminated at twelve oh-five p.m.," said Bill, leaning over to switch off the tape recorder.

* * *

"I'm really excited about this," Josephine told Bill as her heart raced.

"I can't see why – it might be a wild goose chase," Bill replied.

"Listen, the carpet fibres found on the victims match up with those found in Cleves' car, and on his overalls," she began.

"I'm with you so far."

"If Cleves isn't the murderer, then someone else must be carrying the same mix of fibres on his person as Cleves. If this Phil Walker is doing a couple of jobs a week for him, he must have that same mix on his clothes, from the carpets and upholstery," Josephine announced.

"But if he took his overalls off after work, or went to the job in Cleves' van, he wouldn't be taking fibres home with him on his clothes," Bill replied.

"Yes, but can't you see Bill – if he's going home in his own car, the fibres from the carpets are coming off his overalls and attaching themselves to the seat of his car. Then when he goes out in the evening the fibres attach themselves to his *own* clothes. According to Madison the fibres are so minute you wouldn't be able to see them, so he wouldn't brush them off. You heard Cleves say that Walker was laughing and joking with Sheila Jones and her friend, so surely it's possible he bumped into her coming out of the Harbour Fitness Club. If he'd offered her a lift home, she probably wouldn't have refused. She met him at Jane Myers' house, so would have assumed that he was quite safe. I think he must have quite a way with women, and that's why Jane Fielding took him home."

"I can see your reasoning Josephine, but you're assuming he's our man – it may just all be coincidence," Bill told her.

"Well, there's only one way to find out, Bill, let's get over to his address."

* * *

They decided against contacting Walker by telephone in case he was the man responsible for the murders, and drove straight to the fairly remote spot he lived in.

"Forewarned is forearmed, we'll just surprise him," Bill said as the police cars pulled up outside the detached house in a country lane. About a mile away was the ferry crossing to Dartmouth. The nearest neighbour's house was at least quarter of a mile down the lane.

They had decided to take backup, in case it was needed, so inside one of the cars were Josephine, Bill and DC Roger Barnes. The other car contained two PCs.

"Not a bad property for someone who's supposed to be on the dole and doing casual work to make ends meet," Bill commented, as he looked at the house. "I don't think you ought to come up to the front door with us – you'll be safer staying in the car," he advised Josephine.

"We don't even know if he's the man we're after. Even if he is, I don't see how he can do me any harm with you lot here," she replied.

Josephine detailed the two PCs to cover the back of the property while she went up to the front door with Bill and DC Barnes and rang the bell. After several minutes of constant bell ringing no-one had answered the door.

"I don't think he's here," Bill said, peering through the front window into the lounge.

"We'll go in round the back, even if we have to break the door down," Josephine instructed them.

"We don't have a warrant, ma'am," Barnes stated.

"I'm aware of that fact, Barnes," she snapped.

"It's called breaking and entering," Bill added.

"What in the name of God is wrong with you pair? This could be the serial killer we've been pursuing, and I for one am not going to take the risk that while we 'go through the proper channels', this maniac kills again."

"It could also be a completely innocent individual," Bill stated "I mean..."

Josephine interrupted him.

"I will take responsibility for this action. The decision is mine – I'm giving you an order and I expect it to be carried out!"

"Okay, you're the boss," Bill grunted.

They went round to the rear of the house and through a side gate that led into the back garden, where they found the two PCs waiting. The kitchen door faced onto the back garden, and was a traditional half-glazed affair with glass louvres.

"See if you can get in through here without causing too much damage," she told the PCs.

One of the PCs must have had criminal genes. With worrying ease he slid one of the louvre out of the bottom of the window, slid his hand through and unlocked the door from the inside.

"Neatly done lad," Bill said, "Been practising, have we?"

"No sir, my Mum's always locking herself out, and she's got the same sort of door as this."

"Well, let's put our gloves on before we go in,"

Josephine told them.

"I can just see this poor sod coming home to find his house full of coppers. It's enough to give anyone a heart attack," Bill grumbled.

"*If* he's innocent and *if* we do a good enough job he'll never know, will he?" said Josephine angrily. She gave Bill a hard stare that convinced him that discretion was the better part of valour and he resolved to keep his mouth shut for the foreseeable future.

The kitchen was drab and tatty, fitted out with old-fashioned pale blue cupboards with frosted glass panels in the top. The kitchen led into a lounge, again dismal and drab. The majority of the room was dominated by a black leather button-back settee, opposite an ancient Cannon Gas Miser fire. At the far end of the room there was a desk with an office chair, and on top of the desk was a computer.

"There's no way he could have sent mail from a web browser on that – it's far too old, a 286 at best. He'd need at least a 486 to do what he's been doing," DC Barnes said.

"We never thought he was using his own PC – otherwise we could have tracked him. He's been using a cyber café, library or even a night course at the University to get access," Josephine replied.

"Let's take a look upstairs," Bill suggested.

As they entered the large bedroom at the front

of the house they stopped and stared in shock and amazement. Every piece of wall space was covered in pinned up newspaper cuttings. On one wall there were articles and press reports about Josephine's past cases. One headline among many read: 'TEDDY BEAR SERIAL KILLER STALKS TORBAY', and beneath it was an interview with Josephine. Another headline read 'BLAKE SOLVES PUBLISHING HOUSE MURDERS' with a picture of Josephine prominently displayed. Another cutting showed her being presented with a medal for bravery in 1995.

"My God! He's been following your career for years, by the look of these!" Bill exclaimed.

Josephine was intrigued, and at the same time sickened and frightened by the thought of someone so obsessed with her and her work.

"Look at this, ma'am," Barnes said as he pointed to a photograph of Josephine and Jessica leaving her house.

"Jesus, this must have been taken about a week ago! To think he was that close to me!" she shuddered.

"This wall might be reserved for you, ma'am, but just take a look over here," one of the PCs said.

They all turned around. The opposite wall was covered with pictures of Jack The Ripper – artists' impressions that had been printed in newspapers in the 1880s, and pictures of his victims, obviously cut out of books on the subject. Underneath the pictures of his victims there were hand-written details of their horrific injuries.

One cutting was from Police News, an illustrated weekly published in 1888, with an artists impression of the first victim, Polly Nichols, and also pictures of the police and doctors. The headline read 'REVOLTING AND MYSTERIOUS MURDER OF WOMAN IN BUCKS ROW, WHITECHAPEL.'

"God, listen to this, gruesome or what," Bill said and began to read an extract from The Lancet, dated September 1888 that was pinned to the wall.

"... the abdomen had been entirely laid open, and the intestines severed from their mesenteric attachments, had been lifted out of the body and placed on the shoulders of the corpse; whilst the pelvis and uterus and its appendages, with the upper portion of the vagina had been entirely removed. No trace of these parts could be found."

"For heaven's sake Bill, I can read. There's no need to recite it like a bloody speech," she said shakily, as she got out her mobile phone and started to dial.

"Who are you calling?" Bill asked.

"I want to get Andrew and David Burke here right away to look at this. We'll get the forensic team as well – we'll need a full analysis of everything in the house," she looked around at them. "And by the way, have you put that window back, lad?"

"Yes ma'am."

"Good. We found the back door unlocked, alright?"

They muttered their assent.

When she had made her calls Josephine turned to DC Barnes and the PCs and said "I want you to carry out a full search of the property – see if you can find the murder weapons, or any other incriminating evidence."

"Christ, look at this!" Bill exclaimed.

Josephine was almost afraid to look at him.

"Not more sick details, I don't know if I can stand much more," she announced.

In a corner of the room there were photos of Jane Fielding's body, handcuffed to her bed, and of Sheila Jones' mutilated body.

"He must have taken this one before he stuffed her into the sack and dumped it at the back of the barber's shop," Bill said.

"This is worse than the Chamber of Horrors – I've never seen anything so terrible," Josephine said in despair.

"What worries me is that he could return home at any time. I'll get PC Carter to keep a look out in the garden and we need to get full back up,"

Bill said.

"I don't think we need back up Bill, there's five of us, I'm certain we could handle him if he comes back," Josephine replied.

"I don't know that anyone could handle this maniac, and we don't even know what he looks like. See if you can find anything with a picture of him – a passport, driver's licence, anything," he told Barnes.

Bill continued to look at the newspaper articles and cutting on the walls. Josephine tried to get his attention, but he didn't seem to notice her.

"Bill, have you gone deaf?" she asked.

"Er... No, I'll be with you in a minute," he replied, not turning round. His eyes were transfixed by a photograph fixed to the wall. *'She mustn't see this,'* he thought as he tried to remove the photograph from the wall. Josephine walked over to where he was standing. He turned and grabbed her shoulder.

"I think we've seen enough, don't you?" he said as he led her away.

"What's the matter?" she said, pushing him to one side. She examined the place on the wall Bill had been looking at so intently. There was a photograph of herself coming down the steps of the Law Courts, after her divorce hearing. She was wearing her sunglasses in the picture. Drawn on the photograph with what looked like red felt tip was a knife, pointing at her body. Underneath it was written in large red capitals:

MY HANDS ARE COLD
MY HEART IS COLDER STILL
GOD HAS PLACED ME HERE TO KILL
YOUR ULTIMATE CASE IS TO CATCH ME
AND IF YOU FAIL SO SHALL IT BE
WE SHALL DIE TOGETHER
JOSEPHINE AND ME
AND JOIN JACK
AND BE THREE

Josephine's heart pounded in her chest as she read the sick poem written by the deranged killer. She started to feel faint and was just about to fall, when Bill caught her and sat her down on a nearby chair. He put her head between her knees.

"Come on Jo, you'll be okay, we've got him now," he said gently.

After a minute or so she began to recover. She raised her head slowly and looked up at him.

"God Bill, thank heavens we've found him in time, or I dread to think what would have happened."

"Well, we haven't actually got him yet, but we shall do when he returns home, he's bound to come back this evening."

A PC walked over to them.

"I think you should come and look at this,

Sarge."

Josephine remained in the chair, while Bill followed the PC. In a bottom drawer in a large chest in the next room the PC had found a large box, lined with red velvet. When Bill opened it he found it contained six long antique knives.

"They look sharp – and expensive," Bill commented. "A nice set of blades. It's difficult to tell what their original purpose was – household or surgeon's knives. But they've been well looked after, and sharpened with great skill. I'd say we've found our murder weapons. Only one thing worries me." He looked into the recesses of the box.

"There seems to be one missing."

* * *

About twenty minutes later Andrew Blythe arrived, directed upstairs by the PC who'd welcomed him. He ran into the bedroom and quickly inspected the photographs, press cuttings and pictures on the wall. He didn't seem as shocked as the others had been, even when he saw the wall with Josephine's cuttings on it, and the graffitied picture of her. He had been expecting something similar.

He crossed the room to where Josephine was still sitting. She looked pale and drawn. He put his arms around her.

"It's nearly over now Jo. This must have been awful for you to see, but you've found the beast's lair now, and to be honest it's very much as I'd expected. The clippings are a bit of a shock – it looks as if he's been collecting them for years, but we already knew he was obsessed with you and the Ripper. Try to think of it as an act of fate – it could have been anyone in the public eye who became the focus of his obsession. If you can, think of it as being in a narrowly averted accident."

"This is the worst," Josephine said, pointing to the photograph of her leaving the courts, and the graffiti underneath it.

Blythe stared at the picture. As he'd seen it a shudder of real dread had run up his spine. He was used to the company of monsters – it was his business – but when they got close to those you loved, it left you feeling as shocked and appalled as the greenest rookie. He controlled his reactions, so as to not disturb Josephine any further. He could see that the uncertainty of the recent past, and her overwhelming sense of responsibility for the killings had taken its toll on her usually stable character.

"I don't think there's any point in you staying here. Forensic know what's to be done and Burke should be here soon. One of the PCs can drive you back to the station."

"But I want to be here when he returns," Josephine protested.

"Well, I'm not going to let you," Andrew said firmly.

"You can't tell me what to do. I'm a detective inspector and you're just a forensic psychologist!"

"A forensic psychologist who's in love with you, and you're not stopping here! You've got plenty of time to see him when he's arrested and behind bars!" He drew Josephine to him and kissed her passionately. He didn't seem in any way self-conscious even though Barnes and Bill Hughes were staring at them, wry smiles on their lips.

"Right, DC Barnes. Will you take DI Blake back to the station?"

"Certainly, sir," Barnes replied.

Bill waited for Josephine to protest further, but to his amazement she stood up and said

"Okay Andrew, you've made your point. I suppose you're right." Even though she had complied with his wishes she still took charge of the situation. "Right Bill, let's get the squad cars out of sight. If he sees this lot when he returns he'll be doing the biggest runner of all time. I still think you need more backup in case he decides to make a fight of it."

"Don't worry, I'll sort it all out straight away," Bill assured her. He looked at his watch. "It's four o'clock now, he could be here anytime in the next couple of hours, but I'd guess it'll be late this evening. In any case, we'll just wait until he returns."

"I'll report the situation to the Chief – keep in touch," she said.

"That goes without saying – the moment we have him you'll be informed. We'll put an all points out for him as well – we'll get the details of his car and so on, from Cleves."

Thanks Bill," she said. She smiled at Andrew and squeezed his hand, before turning to leave with DC Barnes.

After she'd left Bill turned to Andrew. He was beginning to like this man, despite his earlier misgivings about him.

"Some woman you've got there," he told Blythe.

"I know. I can't see why Tom let her go. *I* never will," he replied.

* * *

On the way back to the station, Josephine's mind was in turmoil. It hadn't bothered her in the least that she'd acquiesced to Andrew's request. Had he said the same thing in different circumstances she'd have probably been furious with him. As a member of the Forensic Psychology department he had no jurisdiction over CID – well, no jurisdiction, period, really. In this case she had done as he requested because she knew he was concerned for her safety and, if she was honest with herself, because she was exhausted. They'd both known they were dealing with an obsessive and dangerous killer, but the horrific findings at his house had knocked the last bit of stuffing out of her. If she was really honest with herself, she had no relish for confronting the madman at all. There would be plenty of time for that when he was under lock and key. She hadn't wanted to burden her team with her fear and apprehension, and so was glad that Andrew had made the decision for her.

* * *

"Marvellous news, DI Blake, marvellous. Well done," the Chief said when she informed him of their grisly discoveries. "But we haven't actually caught him yet?"

"That's correct sir. We've got total covert surveillance of his house, and an APB out for him and his car. Bill Hughes is trying to locate where he would have been today from his sometime employer. We have to tread carefully so as not to forewarn him. It's quite difficult, because his house is located in a fairly remote spot – the nearest house is five hundred yards away, and it's mostly flat around there. Not much cover."

"Hmm," he said, rubbing his chin, "I can see that would present difficulties."

"By a stroke of luck there's a copse of trees just behind his house. I've instructed them to park the cars there."

"And you say the whole house was covered in newspaper clippings, writing and pictures?"

"The bedroom walls were, sir," she replied, and went on to explain all the content of the articles they'd found on the walls.

"It must have been daunting and a little unnerving to see photographs of yourself amongst them?" the Chief suggested.

"You could say that, sir. Especially when I came across a photograph of me that he must have taken quite recently, with a knife drawn across it, and a sick verse beneath, the meaning of which was quite clear. He intends to take my life!"

"There's no chance of that happening now, Inspector. You're quite safe. It's just a matter of sitting tight and waiting for them all to return with him." The Chief smiled, trying to put her mind at rest.

"The Forensic team are there, and I've asked Bill Hughes to make sure they take a video as well as photographs. I hope they manage to get it all done before he returns," she said, glancing at her watch. It was nearly six.

"I'll just ring Bill on his mobile to check on the position," she said.

"Of course, go ahead."

She picked up the phone on his desk and dialled the number. When she heard the phone being picked up she said "Bill, it's me, anything happened?"

"No, quiet as a mouse at the moment. The Forensic team have almost finished. We're all on tenterhooks waiting for the son of a bitch to return. The trouble is we don't have any idea *when* he might return and we're all starving!"

"Trust you to think of your stomach, even at a time like this," Josephine remarked. "Anyway, keep me up to date."

The Chief gestured to Josephine to pass the phone to him. She handed it to him and left the office.

"Chief Inspector Cunningham here. I'm on my way over to you. I'll bring food and some cans from the canteen. Now, you'd better tell me the discreet way to get there. Can I approach from the back, through this copse DI Blake has been telling me about?"

"Oh… right, thanks Sir. Yes, you can come in on a parallel road and walk across the fields. I'll pass you on to Andrew Blythe – he knows the area round here like the back of his hand."

"Thank you Sergeant. DI Blake has left my

office – I didn't want her to know, in case she wanted to come back with me. This business has taken a terrible toll on her – would have taken a terrible toll on any officer. I'll be with you in about forty-five minutes. Now you'd better put on Andrew Blythe to give me directions"

After he had finally hung up, Bill turned to address the team,

"The Chief's on his way over!"

"Oh… No!" they all moaned.

"There is some good news," Bill added. "He's bringing food from the canteen with him."

* * *

Josephine returned to her office. She went to her computer and checked her email, but there were no new messages.

'So, you're not getting in touch today. Well, you'll have a bloody shock when you get home, you sick bastard,' she thought.

DC Sally Jones entered the office.

"I suppose you've heard?" Josephine said.

"Yes, exciting isn't it?" she replied.

"You wouldn't have thought that if you'd been there. It was terrible," Josephine told her, and went on to briefly outline what they'd found.

"You'll be able to see the photographs when we get them from forensics," Josephine told her.

"Don't you mind missing out on all the action?" Sally asked.

"Oddly enough, no. I just want us to put him away forever. I almost wish there was still a death penalty."

When Sally had gone she sifted through some paperwork. She felt tense, edgy and unable to concentrate. *'This is useless,'* she thought, *'I'm going home.'*

Chapter 25

JOSEPHINE PULLED UP outside her house just as it was beginning to rain. A PC was sitting in a car outside as usual. She knocked on the window and he wound it down.

"I suppose you've heard they're all at the suspect's house waiting for him, so there's not much point in you stopping."

"I have to – orders, ma'am."

"Okay. I'm going to take a nap now. I'll bring you a drink out later."

She went into the house and poured herself a brandy. Kicking off her shoes, she laid on the sofa. She couldn't erase the picture of herself with the knife drawn across it from her memory, no matter how she tried to distract herself. Her temples throbbed as the poem revolved in her head.

She decided to take two painkillers, washed

them down with the brandy and lay back down on the sofa. She closed her eyes and the pain gradually started to subside as the tablets took effect. She dozed off into a restless sleep, haunted by dream images of her day.

She awoke suddenly, and realised someone was knocking on the door. She sat up suddenly, her head swimming and glanced at her watch. It was half past eight and the room was swathed in darkness.

"Hang on, I'm coming," she shouted as she switched on the table lamp and walked unsteadily to the front door.

It was a different PC at the door.

"PC Roberts has had to go home ma'am – some sort of emergency. I've taken over from him. I just thought I'd check you were alright. The house was in darkness, you see. I thought I saw someone go into the back garden, but I've checked and there's no-one there," he told her.

"I'd fallen asleep, I'm afraid, that's why you didn't see any lights."

"Well I didn't mean to disturb you, ma'am, but you know what the Chief's like. If he thought I wasn't doing my job properly while on duty… I'll get back to the car now."

"I'm going to have something to eat. Would you like to join me?"

"I'd be honoured ma'am, if it's not too much trouble."

"It's only coffee and sandwiches, I'm afraid."

"Thank you then, ma'am. I'll just have a look round to make sure everything's alright while you get it ready. I'll be back shortly."

Josephine went into the kitchen and prepared a pot of coffee. The PC came back about five minutes later.

"Everything seems okay, and I've radioed the station."

"If there's any action going on tonight it won't be here. It'll be at the suspect's house where my team are waiting," she told him as she placed a plate of sandwiches and the pot of coffee on the table.

"Help yourself," she said. The phone rang, and as she answered it she heard the reassuring tones of Bill Hughes' voice.

"Hi, I just thought I'd keep you up to date. Nothing's happened, except for the surprise appearance of Roger Cleves. He was feeling guilty about giving us Phil Walker's address. The silly bugger had come to warn him. I sent him home."

"I hope you told him not to say anything if he sees him before he returns."

"Don't worry, Mr Cleves won't be talking to anyone after I finished with him. I told him if he so much as opened his mouth to the wrong person I'd charge him with aiding and abetting a murderer. He won't be saying anything to anyone!"

"Is the Chief still there?"

"What do you think! The old fool thought he'd fooled you, and you'd never guess why he wanted to speak to me on the phone. He's driving us all mad. To be honest..." Bill's voice dipped so as not to be overheard "...I think he's going home soon. He's fed up hanging around. He's not used to it like the rest of us. He's only used to sitting behind his desk, giving orders."

"Okay, I'll talk to you later Bill," she said and put down the receiver.

* * *

As they were drinking coffee, having made short work of the sandwiches, she asked the PC how long he'd been in the force.

"Just two years ma'am."

"Do you think you'll stick it?"

"I think so. Despite this recent case, the crime here isn't as bad as in the cities. Although my girlfriend still worries."

Josephine looked at him. He seemed too old to have only been in the force for two years.

"I've followed *your* cases though, ma'am."

"Really? That's interesting."

"Do you think you'll catch this Ripper murderer?"

"I hope so. We know who he is – it's just a matter of time before we get him."

"Mind you ma'am, in a funny sort of way you've almost got to admire him. He's given us all a run for our money," he said, an edge creeping into his voice. He removed his flat cap, and Josephine was able to see his face clearly for the first time. She felt oddly nervous and apprehensive. His eyes seemed to be looking straight through her – dark, menacing evil eyes. In her head she overlaid the photofit of the suspect. The doorman had done a better job than he thought. In a sudden revelation she realised the man opposite her *was* the Ripper killer.

'It's him. My God, it's bloody well him!' she thought, her heart pounding, *'I mustn't let him know I suspect.'*

"More coffee?"

"Yes please, ma'am," he replied.

She lifted the pot, shaking slightly. *'He mustn't see my fear or know I suspect.'*

"I wish this rain would stop," she said as she filled the cup.

He came up behind her.

"I'll put the dishes in the sink for you."

Intense fear was welling up inside her, like an oil gusher building pressure to explode. She knew if he had the slightest inkling she suspected who he was, it would be the end.

The phone in the lounge started an insistent ringing. He walked towards it, but didn't pick it up. He watched her as she answered it, like a biologist observing the amusing behaviour of some new bug.

It was Andrew's voice.

"Josephine, are you okay? I'm just leaving the house. He hasn't come back yet – no sign of him."

"That's great! You've caught him? The press are there? No, I agree – he shouldn't be treated as some kind of hero. I'll come straight over!" she heard her voice babbling as if it were someone else's.

"Jo – are you alright? What the hell's wrong?"

"No – I wouldn't miss it for the world!"

Andrew suddenly realised what she was doing.

"Is he there?" he asked.

"Well, if they think he's a hero…" she replied.

"We'll be over as quickly as we can!" The phone went dead.

Josephine had decided to pretend that they had caught the wrong man. She gambled that it would both disorientate and anger him. In his eyes someone would be getting the credit for his crimes, something impossible for him to accept. She looked up. He was looking out of her front room window into the night, with his back turned to her.

"So, you've got the killer?" he asked.

"Yes, I'm just going to the station now."

Slowly he turned, and she saw the glint of steel in his hands.

"Cut the crap, Josephine, we both know you've got the wrong man! *I'm* the one who committed the murders in Jack's memory. How dare someone else take the credit!"

He advanced across the room to her. Clumsily she backed away. Finally there was nowhere to go. He held the knife to her throat and pushed his face into hers, his mouth working silently.

Josephine steeled herself and stared calmly into his eyes.

"I've seen all your cuttings and pictures. It must have taken you a long time to collect them all?"

"It took *years!* Did you like my poem to you? I used a zoom lens to get the picture. You had no idea I was watching you." He moved the knife and pushed her into a chair.

"You thought you were *so* clever. You'd

solved all your past cases – but you couldn't get me. They didn't catch Jack The Ripper!"

Josephine felt like screaming *'What about you butchering those poor defenceless women you evil, sick bastard?'* She knew her only chance of survival was to keep calm.

"We found out who you are and where you live Jack, or should I say Philip, so we didn't completely fail."

"I'll give you credit for that. How did you find me?"

"From fibres you left on the victims' bodies after you murdered them," she told him

"You're lying! I always wore different clothes each time."

"The fibres you collected on your overalls while doing the carpet cleaning came off on your car seats. And when you went out it didn't matter what clothes you wore – the fibres were transferred back onto them in your car."

"Clever girl. Mind you, you can't take credit for that, can you? They didn't have Forensic Science departments back in Jack's day. Anyway, I've killed four, and you'll be the fifth!"

"There's only been three victims!"

"You're forgetting the gullible young PC who's lying in your back garden with his throat slit. It was *soooo* easy. Everybody loves a uniform, dearie. He thought I'd been sent to help. And help I did."

Josephine lost her calm.

"You murdering bastard! You take lives as if you were swatting flies." She stood up and hit him in the face. He staggered back an inch or so, and grinned.

"That's what I like to see – a bit of spirit. A fight to the finish. *Your* finish." he said, leering at her.

"Jack killed prostitutes – but you kill indiscriminately. He might have been convinced he had a mission, poor mad bastard, but you're just a common or garden thrill killer. You did it to get your kicks, and for no other reason."

"The first one chatted me up in a nightclub – she couldn't wait to get me home. Sheila was chatting me up even though she was married with a child! The last one was a prostitute! I watched her having sex with a customer before I slit her throat."

"She was a student doing it to make ends meet – she didn't deserve to die. You're no reincarnation of Jack The Ripper – you're just a sick social inadequate killing for pleasure. Look at you. Where do your crimes equate to his? The only thing you got right was the first two dates – even then you got the details wrong

– Polly Nichols wasn't strangled, her throat was cut, and the killer didn't have sex with her first. This isn't about *Jack* – it's just *you!*"

His face purpled with rage.

"You don't belong in any murderer's hall of fame – you belong in a madhouse, you sad bastard!" Josephine continued to shout.

"I'm not mad – I'm clever," he said, advancing towards her.

"I copied Jack's crimes and fooled *you,* Miss Bloody-Clever-Detective. You couldn't even trace my messages. *You're* the mad ones – sitting in that house waiting for me to come home. And where am I? I'm *here,*" he lunged at her.

"Killing *you!*"

He grabbed Josephine and threw her across the room.

"So, who's the clever one?"

Her head hit the corner of the wall, causing a wave of pain and nausea to break across her consciousness. She hauled herself up, grabbed an ornament from the table and threw it at him. It served to stop his headlong rush at her, giving her enough time to make a break for the kitchen. He threw himself at her ankles and she fell to the floor, halfway through the kitchen doorway, the impact driving all the breath from her body. She felt a streak of cold fire run down her arm, followed by a wet, warm feeling, and realised he'd slashed her. She screamed, suddenly and loudly, and kicked at him frantically. She felt her shoe make contact with something soft that gave – *'His mouth!'* she thought, with satisfaction. He grunted in pain and released her momentarily. She dragged herself up by the door jamb and turned round towards him as he slashed out again with the blade. The blade flashed past her stomach, just cutting the material of her sweater. She drew back her foot and kicked him viciously between the legs.

He dropped the knife as he bought his hands to his tortured groin, and Josephine heard it skitter away across the polished linoleum of the kitchen floor. From somewhere outside Josephine could hcar police sirens. Her only thought was to get to a place of safety. She ran to the hall and up the stairs. From the corner of her eye she spotted Philip Walker pushing himself back to his feet. He almost visibly shook off the terrible pain from his groin and began to look for the knife.

The sirens were closer now.

The banister felt slippery because of the blood gushing from Josephine's arm. Her shock and terror were greater than her pain, as she desperately tried to keep her balance. She felt disorientated as she lurched into the bedroom and tried to drag the chest of drawers in front of the door. Her strength was waning now – she could barely move it. The bedroom door exploded inward, throwing the chest of drawers across the room. Philip Walker stood framed in the doorway, any pretence to rationality now gone.

"*Heeeere's Jack!*"

Somewhere at the periphery of her hearing she heard Andrew Blythe shouting "Quick, break the bloody door down!" and heard a crash. But by then the beast she had fought for so long was upon her.

"You can't get away my sweet! Accept your fate and we'll join Jack together!"

She felt another lance of cold fire pierce her heart, and looked down. His knife protruded from her chest. Above her he was laughing, part cackle, part gurgle.

'So this is what it feels like to die' she thought, and a shaft of pain shot through her tortured body. She convulsed to meet it. Philip had pulled the blade from her, and as her head turned to meet his eyes he bought it swiftly across his own throat. A warm fountain of his blood arced across her body and face, followed by the heavy weight of his body dropping on hers. As consciousness fled she felt a small surge of satisfaction.

'Burn in hell you bastard. Burn in hell.'

'Burn in hell.'

Blythe got to the doorway just in time to see Walker cut his own throat and fall onto Josephine. The tension of the drive there and the half lit house gave the scene the quality of nightmare. The paramedics behind him crossed the room and dragged Walker's body off Josephine. One of the paramedics went to Walker.

"Leave that scum – just see to her!" Andrew shouted.

He wanted so terribly to hold her, but they wouldn't let him near her. She was being cocooned in tubes and bandages. Behind him one of the team was preparing a stretcher for her as two paramedics desperately tried to staunch the bleeding chest wound.

"I think we're losing her."

"No, I've got a pulse, but she's got to be stabilised before she's moved."

It took ten agonising minutes of Andrew Blythe's life to transfer her to the ambulance. In the meantime another team had arrived and worked on Philip Walker. They were unable to save him, and pronounced him dead.

"I can't lose her," Andrew said, as he sat in the back of the ambulance. He held her hand. It was cold and her lips were turning blue.

"She's lost so much blood that she's going into shock. Her only hope is a transfusion, but I doubt we'll get there in time," the paramedic told him.

"Come on Jo," Andrew whispered in her ear, "Hang on, you've got to make it, I can't live without you."

The ambulance pulled out of the driveway, its blue lights flashing, escorted by two police motorcycles.

Josephine opened her eyes and said feebly,

"I can't fight any longer Andrew. He's won." Her eyes closed slowly.

"No... no... you must hang on Jo! You must..." He sobbed like a child as he held her hand.

"Don't write me off – I'll be back."

If you have enjoyed this book you will be certain to enjoy these other titles by Janet Harward

THE TEDDY BEAR MURDERS

Detective Inspector Josephine Blake and her team are on the track of a pyschopathic serial killer who leaves a teddy bear at the scene of the crime.

With her family life in turmoil Josephine tries to outwit the sadistic killer, as Devon is gripped in a vice of terror and mayhem.

"In the best of traditions we are kept guessing to the end."

–Herald Express

"A traditional whodunnit with plenty of red herrings and crooked twists."

–Birmingham Evening Mail

AVAILABLE AT ALL GOOD BOOKSHOPS

THE TEDDY BEAR MURDERS

IN MEMORY OF MURDER

A tranquil Spanish church is thrown into chaos when Andrew Markham's face and hair become a blazing mass of flames and molten wax...

In Devon, Detective Inspector Josephine blake and her team are searching for a perverted serial killer, as young girls are being held hostage for days, enduring horrible torture before being murdered...

Meanwhile across the country members of the literary establishment are dying in what seem to be a series of gruesome accidents...

Can these events possibly be related?

"The plot is gripping to the end, with Blake under scrutiny from those above her, who doubt that the roles of woman and copper can be combined"

– *Crime Time*

IN MEMORY OF MURDER